"I'm not supposed to like you, Kincaid," she whispered against his collar. "I'm not supposed to even know you."

"I know."

Liza's fresh, angelic face, momentarily free of attitude or suspicion, was smiling.

Those peachy lips were parted in anticipation, and, like a hungry man, Holden couldn't resist. He leaned in, brushed his lips against hers. Her taste was sweeter than he'd imagined.

The scrape of metal on metal ___ ___ Holden from the une___ ___ ___ ___ t kiss, reminding ___ ___ ___ ___ ___ ne of it—that he ___ ___ ___ ___ e for them both ___ ___

JULIE MILLER

PRIVATE S.W.A.T. TAKEOVER

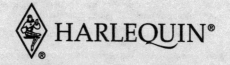

HARLEQUIN®

TORONTO • NEW YORK • LONDON
AMSTERDAM • PARIS • SYDNEY • HAMBURG
STOCKHOLM • ATHENS • TOKYO • MILAN • MADRID
PRAGUE • WARSAW • BUDAPEST • AUCKLAND

For the Greyhound Museum in Atchison, Kansas.
What a pleasure to meet "The Talented Mr. Ripley," a retired
champion greyhound, and his two female companions, who
greeted us at the door, kept us company as we toured the facility
and insisted that we pet them.

Thanks to the friendly docents and dog owners who made the visit
an unexpected yet marvelous addition to last summer's vacation.
And thank you to every person with a kind heart and a conscience
who rescues unwanted, discarded and neglected animals
and gives them a loving home.

ISBN-13: 978-0-373-69357-3
ISBN-10:   0-373-69357-5

PRIVATE S.W.A.T. TAKEOVER

ABOUT THE AUTHOR

Julie Miller attributes her passion for writing romance to all those fairy tales she read growing up, and to shyness. Encouragement from her family to write down all those feelings she couldn't express became a love for the written word. She gets continued support from her fellow members of the Prairieland Romance Writers, where she serves as the resident "grammar goddess." This award-winning author and teacher has published several paranormal romances. Inspired by the likes of Agatha Christie and Encyclopedia Brown, Ms. Miller believes the only thing better than a good mystery is a good romance.

Born and raised in Missouri, she now lives in Nebraska with her husband, son and smiling guard dog, Maxie. Write to Julie at P.O. Box 5162, Grand Island, NE 68802-5162.

CAST OF CHARACTERS

Holden Kincaid—The youngest Kincaid brother, he's a S.W.A.T. sharpshooter with an eye for whatever he lines up in his sights—including an obstinate redhead who can identify his father's killer. As her self-proclaimed protector, surviving close proximity with the quirky beauty may be as tough as surviving, period.

Liza Parrish—This spunky redheaded veterinary student seems to get along better with the animals she rescues than with most people. She's willing to come forward and help KCPD find a cop killer. But a glitch in her memory—and a ruthless hit man who wants her dead—stand in the way of justice.

Mr. Smith—Code name for an assassin who won't tolerate loose ends.

William Caldwell—Mourning for his best friend has brought him closer to that best friend's widow.

Detective Kevin Grove—The investigator assigned to the Kincaid murder.

Dr. Trent Jameson—Psychologist specializing in hypnotherapy.

Bruiser, Cruiser & Yukon—Three survivors.

Z Group—A covert organization disbanded at the end of the Cold War. Its former operatives are being silenced one by one.

Deputy Commissioner John Kincaid—His unsolved murder haunts his four sons.

Prologue

April

"…'Tis I'll be here in sunlight or in shadow. Oh Danny Boy, Oh Danny Boy…"

Officer Holden Kincaid had learned three things from his father—how to sing like an Irish tenor, how to shoot straight and how to be a man.

He'd never learned how he was supposed to deal with losing the father he idolized to two bullets. He'd never learned how he was supposed to help his mother stop weeping those silent tears that twisted him inside out. He'd never learned why good men had to die while bastards like the ones who'd kidnapped, beaten and murdered Deputy Commissioner John Kincaid could cozy up someplace safe and warm while Holden buried his father in the cold, hard ground.

The lyrics flowed, surprisingly rich and full from his throat and chest, while he sought out his fractured family. Thank God his brother, Atticus, was here to sit with their mother and hold her up throughout this long, arduous day. Though he was the hardest one to shake of all the Kincaids, Atticus was hurting, too. Holden noted the way his unflappable older brother sat, with his hand over his badge and heart, revealing a chink in his stoic armor.

He looked farther back and spotted Sawyer standing just outside the tent, getting soaked. The tallest of all the Kincaid brothers, Sawyer might be hanging back so as not to block anyone's view of the graveside ceremony. Judging by the way he kept shifting from foot to foot, though, it was more likely he was scanning the crowd of mourners, sizing everyone up as a potential suspect. Holden could understand that. He was about to crawl out of his own skin because he was so antsy to do something about the injustice of their father's murder.

But Susan Kincaid had asked him to sing. Had asked him to honor his father with John Kincaid's favorite song. He'd suck up his own grief and anger, and do whatever he had to do to bring their mother some measure of peace and comfort.

Speaking of comfort, where the hell was Edward? Holden's oldest brother should be here, too, no matter what the reclusive master detective was dealing with. Yeah, he knew that there were a couple of heartwrenching reasons why Mount Washington Cemetery was the last place Edward might want to be. But after losing the husband she'd loved for more than thirty-seven years, all her sons gathered around her might be the one thing that could bring a smile back to their mother's face. For her sake, if not his own, Edward Kincaid needed to be with the family.

Holden finished the song, as quietly as a prayer, and blinking away his own tears as he pulled his KCPD hat from beneath his arm and placed it over his light brown hair, he turned to the flag-draped casket to salute his father. The steady drumbeat of rain on the green awning over the burial site punctuated the ensuing silence like a death knell. Holden didn't even remember moving, but next thing he knew, he was seated beside his mother, warming her chilled fingers in his grasp. The Commissioner of Police completed the eulogy and the twenty-one gun salute resonated through every bone in his body.

And then it was done.

Or was it all just beginning?

"Holden?" Atticus asked him to take his place at their mother's side. Instead of telling him the reason, he nodded toward a copse of trees about thirty yards up the sloping hill.

Son of a gun. Edward had shown up, after all. He wasn't wearing his KCPD dress uniform like the rest of them, but even from this distance Holden could tell he'd cleaned up, and, hopefully, sobered up to pay his respects to their father.

Holden was twenty-eight years old and he still had the urge to charge up that hill and swallow Edward up in a bear hug. But he'd let wiser heads prevail. Namely, Atticus. Charging and hugging would probably send Ed running in the opposite direction just as fast as his cane and gimpy leg would allow.

With his extensive training in Special Weapons and Tactics, Holden understood that teamwork usually got the job done better than any one man's heroic gesture. Tamping down his own desire to take action, Holden slid into the role required of him on this particular mission. He drew his mother's hand into the crook of his arm. "I'll stick with her."

As Atticus picked up an umbrella and went to talk with Edward, Susan Kincaid's grip shifted. "You did a beautiful job, sweetie."

"Glad to do it, Mom. I know Dad loved that song. He taught it to me on one of our camping trips. Scared all the fish away with our singing. All the brothers, too."

He heard a bit of a laugh. Good. Maybe not.

He easily supported her weight as she wrapped her arm more tightly through his and leaned her cheek against his shoulder. As he looked down at the crown of her dark brown hair, he noticed gray sprinkled through the rich sable color. Hell. He hadn't noticed those before. He'd bet good money the sudden sign of aging hadn't been there a week ago when he'd stopped over for a family dinner—while his father had still been alive.

An unexpected rage at the collateral damage the senseless murder had spawned exploded through every cell in his body. John Kincaid's killer hadn't just stolen his life. The killer had left a big hole in the leadership of the Kansas City Police Department, and an even bigger hole in the hearts of the Kincaid family.

Somebody had to pay for all that.

But with the same kind of deep breath that iced his nerves before he pulled the trigger to shoot, Holden buried his anger. Instead of lashing out, he leaned over and pressed a kiss to the crown of Susan's hair. "I love you, Mom."

She hugged the triangular folded flag tight to her chest and nodded, rubbing her cheek against his sleeve. The sniffle he heard was the only indicator of sadness she revealed. Her brown eyes were bright and shining when she looked up at him and shared a serene smile. "I love you, too, sweetie." Then she settled in at his side, holding her chin up at a proud angle his father would have admired. "Walk me to the car?"

"You bet."

They were all the way down to the road when a man in an expensive black suit stopped them. "Su?"

"Bill."

Holden adjusted the umbrella to keep his mother covered as William Caldwell, his father's best friend since their fraternity days at college, bent down to exchange a hug. The laugh lines alongside his mouth had deepened into grooves, emphasizing his silvering hair and indicating another casualty of John Kincaid's death.

"Holden." As Bill pulled away, he reached for Holden's hand. "I can't tell either of you how sad, and how angry, this makes me." Releasing them both, he straightened his own black umbrella over his head. "I'm making a sizable donation to the KCPD Benevolence Fund in John's name, but if there's anything more personal I can do… anything…ever…."

Bill Caldwell ran his multinational technology company as smoothly as he'd told B.S. stories around the campfire on the many hunting and fishing trips he'd taken with the Kincaids over the years. But today he seemed to be at a loss for words.

Susan squeezed his hand, rescuing him from his overwhelming emotions. "Come to the house, Bill. We're having an informal potluck dinner. Nothing fancy. I just want to be surrounded by everyone who loved John. I want to celebrate what a good, wonderful man he was."

Bill squeezed back and leaned in to kiss her cheek. "I'll be there."

Holden settled his mother into the back of the black limousine they'd ridden in to the cemetery. After tucking a blanket over her damp legs and finding a box of tissues to set beside her, he closed the door and circled the long vehicle to greet Atticus as he walked up the asphalt road. Alone.

Holden's temper flared again. "Where the hell is Edward?" His long strides took him away from the limo. "You went to talk to him. What did he say?"

As usual, Atticus didn't ruffle. "I talked to him. As tough as this is on us, you have to know it's probably harder for him to be here. His wife and daughter aren't that far from where—"

"I know he's hurting," Holden snapped. "But Mom wants to see him. He can't be such a selfish son of a bitch that he'd cause her pain, can he?"

"Get off your high horse. Sawyer's with him—bringing him around to avoid the crowd. Ed won't let Mom down."

"You don't have to defend me, Atticus." Edward and Sawyer walked out of the woods to the limo. "Got your boxers in a knot, baby brother?"

The rain whipped his face as Holden spun around. Edward's dark hair and beard had been trimmed short— a vast improvement over the shaggy caveman look he'd sported a couple of weeks ago the last time Holden had dropped by his place to try to annoy him out of his drunken grief. Yet there was something dark and sad about his pale gray eyes that wiped away Holden's temper.

He noted the scar cutting through Edward's beard, and the way he seemed to lean heavily on his cane as he approached. Edward had been through more than any man should have to endure, and Holden was immediately contrite about any doubts he'd had about his oldest brother's loyalty to the family.

"Hell." It wasn't much to offer in the way of sympathy, but Holden walked the distance between them and wrapped Edward up in a tight hug. "I miss you."

At first, Edward's shoulders stiffened at the contact. Then one arm closed around Holden's back and squeezed with a familiar strength. But just as quickly as the bond was affirmed, Ed was pushing him away. "Get off me, kid." He inclined his head toward the limo. "Is Mom inside?"

"Yeah."

Edward swiped the rain from his face and looked at Holden, then beyond to Sawyer and Atticus. The four brothers hadn't been united like this for a long time. But the unspoken sentiment between them felt as strong as ever. "This ain't right."

After Edward climbed into the backseat for a few minutes alone with their mother, Holden closed the door and straightened, standing guard to ensure their privacy. Sawyer rested his forearms on the roof of the limo on the opposite side, looking first to Atticus beside him, and then across the top to Holden. "We're gonna get whoever did this, right?"

"Right," Atticus said before turning away to scan the departing crowd and keep everyone else away from the private family meeting.

Holden took the same vow. "Amen."

Chapter One

October

Oh God. In her sleep, Liza Parrish rolled over and tried to wake herself up. It was happening again. And she couldn't stop it.

"Shh, baby. Shush."

Liza closed her hand around the dog's muzzle and hunched down closer beside him in his hiding spot in the shadowy alley. The fact that he didn't protest the silencing touch was evidence of just how close to starvation this furry bag of skin and bones was.

He was lucky she'd come here after classes and work tonight, following up on a call to the shelter about an emaciated stray wandering the dock area that neither the county's Animal Control Unit nor the Humane Society had been able to catch. She'd get him back to the vet's office where she was interning—feed him a little bit of food and water, run some tests to make sure he wasn't infected with heartworm or some other debilitating disease, give him some love and a bath, and maybe just save his life.

But who was going to save her*?*

She hoped the dog was the only one who could hear her heart thumping over the whoosh of the Missouri River, surging past only a few yards away.

Trying to calm herself so the dog wouldn't panic and give away their position, Liza blinked the dampness of the foggy night from her eyelashes. If only she could blink away the stench of wet dog and old garbage just as easily. If only she could blink herself to safety.

Her leg muscles were beginning to cramp in protest against just how long she'd been curled up with the knee-high terrier mix, hiding behind the trash cans and plastic bags that smelled as if they could have been left in this alley off the river docks ever since the warehouses on either side had closed. She was tired, aching, chilled to the bone—and scared out of her mind.

But she wasn't about to move.

Hearing two gun shots from the other side of the brick wall she huddled against did that to a woman.

Watching the two men waiting in the black car parked only ten, maybe twenty feet from her hiding space also kept her rooted to the spot. Her jeans were soaking up whatever oily grime filled the puddle where she crouched. The only warmth she could generate were the hot tears stinging her eyes and trickling down her cheeks.

Was this what it had been like for her parents and for Shasta? Endlessly waiting for death to find her. Fighting back the terror that churned her stomach into an acid bath. Driving herself crazy trying to decide whether, if she was discovered, it was smarter to fight or run for her life.

She felt her parents' terror. Felt her pet's confusion as he valiantly tried to protect them. Felt their senseless loss all over again.

Two gunshots.

Death.

And she had a ringside seat.

The dog squirmed in her arms and Liza absently began to stroke his belly, feeling each and every rib. "Shh, baby." She mouthed the words. She wasn't the only witness to this crime.

Eyewitness.

Almost of their own volition—maybe it was a subconscious survival streak kicking in—her eyes began to take note of the details around her.

Black car. Big model. Missouri plate B*? Or was that an* 8*? Oh hell. She couldn't make out the number without moving.*

But she could see the men inside. She had a clear look at the driver, at least. He was a muscular albino man, with hair as shockingly white as the tattoos twining around his arms and neck were boldly colored. In the passenger seat beside him sat a black man. He was so tall that his face was hidden by the shadows near the roof of the car's interior. She could tell he was built like a lineman because he was having a devil of a time finding room enough to maneuver himself into his suit jacket.

The size of the black man was frightening enough, but the albino looked crazy scary, like he'd beat the crap out of anyone who stared crosswise at him.

She was staring now. Stop it!

Liza closed her eyes and turned away. She could note any damn detail she wanted, but if those crazy colorless eyes spotted her, she was certain there'd be no chance to tell anyone what she'd seen.

The gunshots had rent the air only a couple of minutes ago, but it felt like hours had passed before she heard the next sound. The sticky, raspy grind of metal on metal as someone opened the front door of the warehouse and closed it with an ominous clank behind him. At the sharp bite of heels against the pavement, she opened her eyes again. The black man was getting out of the car with an umbrella, opening the back door.

"No, Liza. Don't look." It was almost as if she could hear her mother's voice inside her head, warning her to turn away from the eyes of a killer. "It'll hurt too much."

"But I need to see," she argued, feeling the tears welling up and clogging her sinuses again. "It's the only way I'll be free of this nightmare."

"Don't look, sweetie. Don't look."

"I have to."

Liza squinted hard, catching sight of the back of a pinstriped suit climbing into the backseat of the car.

"No!" She threw her head back. She'd missed him. She hadn't seen the man who'd fired the gunshots.

The next several minutes passed by in a timeless blur. The car drove away. She'd seen fogged up windows, and a face through the glass. But it had been too vague. Too fast.

She didn't know what the third man looked like.

As she had dreamed so many times before, what happened next was as unclear as the mist off the river that filled the air. But Liza was inside the warehouse now, cradling the weightless black and tan dog in her arms, creeping through the shadows.

If there were gunshots, if there were killers, then there must be....

"Oh, my God."

Liza had no free hand to stifle her shock or the pitying sob that followed.

In the circle of harsh lamplight cast by the bare bulb

hanging over the abandoned office door was a man. Lying in a spreading pool of blood beside an overturned chair, his broken, bruised body had been laid out in a mock expression of reverence. His twisted fingers were folded over his stomach. The jogging suit he wore had been zipped to the neck, and the sleeve had been used to wipe the blood from his face.

"Stay with me, baby." She set the dog on the floor, keeping one foot on the leash she'd looped around his neck in case he should find the energy to try to run from her again. Although she was in grad school learning how to treat animals, not humans, she knelt beside the man's carefully arranged body and placed two shaking fingers to the side of his neck. She already knew he was dead.

"Remember." Liza heard the voice inside her head. Not her own. Not her mother's. "Remember."

"I'm trying."

Barely able to see through her tears, Liza pulled her cell phone from her pocket and turned it on. She punched in 9-1-1. "I need to report a murder."

"Remember."

"Shut up." She tried to silence the voice in her head. She wasn't on the phone anymore. She was kneeling beside the body, reaching out to him.

The dead man's eyes popped open.

Liza screamed. She tried to scoot away. "No!"

His bloody hand caught hers in an ice-cold grip and he jerked his face right up to hers. "Remember!"

"No-o-o!" Liza's own screams woke her from her nightmare. She thrashed her way up to a sitting position. Panting hard, she was barely able to catch her breath. And though she felt the haunting chill of her cursed dreams deep in her soul, she was burning up.

"What the hell? What…"

She became aware of wiping her hands frantically, and then she stilled.

On the very next breath she snatched up the pen and notepad from her bedside table, just as she had been trained to do. Write down every detail she remembered from her dream before the memories eluded her. *Dead body. Cold hand.*

"Remember," she pleaded aloud. Before the body. There were gunshots. She put pen to paper. "Dead man. Two shots." And…and…

Blank.

"Damn it!" Liza hurled the pen and pad across the room into a darkness as lonely and pervasive as the shadows locked up inside her mind.

A low-pitched woof and a damp nuzzle against her hand reminded her she wasn't alone. She was home. She was safe. She flipped on the lamp beside her bed and with the light, her senses returned.

Three sets of eyes stared at her.

She could almost smile. Almost. "Sorry, gang."

The warm, wet touch on her fingers was a dog's nose. She quickly scooped the black and tan terrier mix into her lap and hugged him, scratching his flanks as she rocked back and forth. Liza couldn't feel a single rib on him now. "Good boy, Bruiser. Thanks for taking care of Mama. I'm sorry she scared you."

Not for the first time Liza wondered if the scrappy little survivor remembered that night more clearly than her own fog of a memory allowed her to. She traced the soft white stripe at the top of his head. "I wish you could tell me what we saw. Then we could make this all go away."

But she and her little guardian weren't alone. The

nightmare might have chilled her on the inside, but her legs were toasty warm, caught beneath a couple of quilts and the lazy sprawl of her fawn-colored greyhound, Cruiser. "So I woke you, too, huh?"

Cruiser outweighed Bruiser by a good sixty pounds, and could easily outrun him, but a guard dog she was not. She was the cuddler, the comforter, the pretty princess who preferred to offer the warmth of her body rather than her concern. Liza reached down and stroked the dog's sleek, muscular belly as she rolled onto her back. "I know you're worried, too, deep down inside. I wish I could be as serene and content as you."

And then, of course, there was the furry monster by the door. Yukon's dark eyes reflected the light with something like contempt at the disruption of his sleep. Despite weeks of training and all the patience she could muster, the silvery gray malamute had yet to warm up to her. No amount of coaxing, not even a treat, could lure him to join her in bed with the other dogs. He didn't even mooch when she cooked in the kitchen. Yukon tolerated the rest of the household. He accepted the food and shelter she offered and ran or roller-bladed with her anytime she asked. She always got the feeling that he was looking for a chance to escape—to run and keep on running away from the prison he temporarily called home. No way was Yukon ever going to thank her for rescuing him from being euthanized by an owner who couldn't handle such a big, athletic dog. No way did he care that she'd been scared, trapped in a nightmare she'd relived time and again these past six months. No way was he going to offer one bit of his strength to make her feel any better. She spotted the crumpled notepad lying just a few feet away from him against the wall. "Nothing personal, big guy," she said. "Sorry I woke you."

Liza checked the clock. Four a.m. She'd worked the late shift at the vet clinic and had her applied microbiology review in another four hours. She should try to get some more sleep.

But she was wide awake in the middle of the night. She had no family to call, no arms to turn to for comfort. She was isolated by the very nightmare she desperately needed to share with someone who could help her complete the memories and then get them out of her head. But the KCPD and a restraining order from the D.A.'s office—to keep her identity out of the press—prevented her from talking to anyone but the police and her therapist about the gruesome crime she'd witnessed. She was alone, with no one but her three dogs for company.

She glanced over at Yukon, who was resting his muzzle on his outstretched paws again. *He* understood isolation. "But you like it better than I do, big guy."

With sleep out of the question and class still hours away, Liza shoved Cruiser aside and kicked off the covers. "Move it, princess."

Knowing she'd have extra fur and body heat to keep her warm, Liza kept the house cool at night. The October chill that hung in the air shivered across her skin as her bare feet touched the wood floor beside her bed. Instead of complaining, she let the coolness rouse her even further. After a few deep breaths, she stepped into her slippers and pulled on her robe as she walked past Yukon and headed for the kitchen.

The usual parade followed, with Bruiser right on her heels and Cruiser padding behind at a more leisurely pace. Yukon deigned to rise and come out of the bedroom, only to lie down outside the kitchen doorway. Liza brewed a pot of green tea, ignored her fatigue and pulled out her pharmacology text. She read her next assignment until the first rays of sunlight peeked through the curtains above the kitchen sink.

It was 7 a.m. Late enough to politely make the call she'd been ready to make since the nightmare woke her.

The male voice on the other end of the line cleared the sleep from his throat before answering. "This is Dr. Jameson."

Great. She'd still gotten him out of bed. Now her therapist would think she'd had some kind of breakthrough. But all she had was the same familiar nightmare she wished would go away.

Combing her fingers through the boyish wisps of her copper-red hair, Liza apologized. "I'm sorry to wake you, Doctor. This is Liza Parrish. I think I'm…" She swallowed the hesitation. There was no thinking about this. *Just say it and get on with it, already.* "I want to try the hypnotherapy you suggested. I need to get the memory of that cop's murder out of my head."

"CAN SHE TELL ME ANYTHING NEW or not?" The burly blond detective named Kevin Grove addressed the question across his desk to Dr. Trent Jameson rather than to her.

The gray-haired psychologist answered for her as well. "Possibly. Though she seems to be juxtaposing her parents' deaths with your crime scene, there were certainly a few more details in the account she shared with me this morning. She's certain there were two gunshots now. And that the victim's body had been arranged in a way that indicates the killer—or someone who was on the scene with the killer—cared about him."

"Uh-huh." Grove frowned, looking as skeptical as Liza felt.

Dr. Jameson continued. "I realize those are clues your forensic team can piece together as well. But I tell you, the clarity of her memory is improving. I believe we've reached the point where I can put her under and guide her memories toward a particular fact."

"You can do that? You can pick a specific memory out of her head?" Grove asked.

"It's a new technique I've been working on for several months with some success." Jameson blew out a long sigh, as though defending his expertise was a tedious subject. "I believe questioning Liza while she's in a suggestive state could tap into those memories she's either blocked or forgotten."

"You want to hypnotize her here." Detective Grove still wasn't up to speed on the idea of hypnotherapy. Or else, that doubt in his tone meant he understood just fine what Dr. Jameson was proposing—he just didn't think it was a worthwhile idea.

Liza squirmed in her chair. Surrendering her thoughts and memories to a professional therapist was risky enough. To do it in front of an audience felt a whole lot like standing up on a firing range and letting the entire world take a potshot at her.

But she had to try. This was about more than clearing her head of the nightmares that plagued what little sleep she did get and left her exhausted. She owed something to John Kincaid, the dead man she'd found in the warehouse. Six years ago, witnesses had come forward to help convict the thieves who'd murdered her family in a home invasion. Liza had been away at college, working on her undergraduate degree, the night her parents and pet were murdered. She hadn't been there to fight to protect her family. Or to see anything useful she could testify to at their killers' trial.

But she could testify for John Kincaid. If she could remember.

Helping another victim find justice was the only way she could help her late parents.

Twisting her gloves in her hands, Liza distracted herself from the uneasy task that lay ahead of her by counting the dog hairs clinging to the sleeves of her blue fleece jacket.

"The setting isn't ideal." Dr. Jameson gestured around the busy precinct office with an artistic swirl of his fingers. "But I'm skilled enough to perform my work anywhere I'm needed. A little privacy would be nice, though."

Detective Grove pushed his chair back and stood. "A little privacy sounds good. We can use one of the interview rooms."

Divided up into a maze of desks and cubicle walls, the detectives' division of the Fourth Precinct building was buzzing with indecipherable conversations among uniformed and plain-clothes investigators and the technicians and support staff who worked with them. Liza felt a bit like a rat in a maze herself as she got up and followed Dr. Jameson's fatherly figure and Grove—the bulldog-faced detective who'd interviewed her before in conjunction with the Kincaid murder case.

Liza tucked her gloves into her pockets as they zigzagged between desks. While Dr. Jameson discussed their late morning session with the detective, she couldn't help but compare the two men. Both were eager to tap into the secrets locked inside her brain. But while Detective Grove wasn't concerned with how her memories got tangled up, her therapist seemed to think he could use the painful experience of her parents' deaths to tap into her hazy memory of John Kincaid's murder, and draw out the information that he believed was hiding in a well-protected corner of her mind.

It felt odd to be discussed as though she were a walking, talking clinical experiment instead of a human being with ears and feelings.

About as odd as it felt to be watched by the tall, tawny-haired hotshot standing beside a black-haired man with glasses at the farthest desk.

Liza's first instinct was to politely look away. The two men were obviously sharing a conversation, and the parade through the desks had probably just caught his attention for a moment. But the moment passed and she could feel him still watching her. Liza turned his way again, then nearly tripped over her own feet as she stuttered to a halt. "Impossible," she gasped.

Remember. An imaginary hand from her nightmare grabbed hers and she flinched.

She was being watched by a ghost.

Closing her eyes and shaking the imagined sensation from her fingers, she purged the foolish notion from her head. Her brain was tired and playing tricks on her. Ghosts, shmosts. They weren't real. Taking a deep breath, her streak of self-preservation that had seen her through the most difficult times of her life kicked in, giving her the impetus to mask her shock before opening her eyes and moving on.

Man. Ghost.

Reality. Memory.

She snuck another peek as the man lowered his head to resume his conversation. *See? You twit. Get a grip.*

The similarities were there, yes. But that honey-brown hair wasn't streaked with gray.

The square jaw was whole. Not bruised and broken.

The eyes were blue as cobalt. Piercing. Very much alive.

Liza circled behind a carpeted cubicle wall. No way could Captain Hotshot be the same man she'd found murdered on that warehouse floor. She was going nuts, plain and simple. Agreeing to interrogation under hypnosis was a very bad idea. She should go home. Go back to work. Go for a run with her dogs. Anything normal. Anything physical. Anything that would stop the fear and confusion, and get her life back to its fast-paced, sleep-deprived, business-as-usual state.

But when she cleared the wall, Liza was forced to pause again as a pair of uniformed officers escorted a young man wearing baggy pants to a desk and hand-cuffed him to a chair. Determined to convince her brain that she'd only imagined Kincaid's ghost across the room, Liza used those few camouflaged seconds to study the man who'd spooked her.

The badge hanging from a chain around his neck marked him as a police officer. Yet, unlike the detectives wearing suits and ties or the patrol officers wearing their standard blue uniforms, this man was dressed in black from neck to toe. Black turtleneck. Black gun and holster at his hip. Black pants tucked into what looked like black army boots. And a black flak vest that bore two rows of white letters—*KCPD* and *S.W.A.T.*

Mask the spiky crop of hair with a knit cap and add stripes of eye black beneath his eyes, and she'd think he was ready to launch some kind of covert attack.

Against *her,* judging by the way his gaze darted back to her the instant her path cleared and she took a step.

That nosy son of a... Red-haired temper flamed through her veins, and Liza tilted her chin and hurried after Jameson and Grove.

So Captain Hotshot was a tough guy. One of those S.W.A.T. cops who defused bombs and calmed riots and shot rifles at bad guys from a mile away. He probably hunted for fun—had trophies of innocent deer and hapless pheasants mounted on his walls at home.

Tough guys didn't scare her.

The detective with glasses standing beside him kept talking, but the man in black continued to watch her. Suspecting her own scrutiny might have intensified his, Liza resolutely focused her gaze on the back of Jameson's silvery head and wished the path from Grove's desk to the interview room was straighter and shorter.

She felt the tough guy turn his conversation back to the man beside him, but the instant she snuck a glance over to make sure his fascination with her had waned, he blinked. And when those clear blue eyes opened again, they locked on to hers across the sea of desks and detectives. What the hell? Liza's pulse rate kicked up a notch. Without looking away, he lowered his head to say something to the other man. Were they talking about her?

Liza broke eye contact as she neared his position. A distinct feminine awareness hummed beneath the surge of temper. But both energies fizzled as an all-too-familiar panic crept in. Maybe she had more than her sanity to worry about. Did he recognize her? Did he know why she was here? Dr. Jameson and Detective Grove had reached the hallway leading to the interview rooms. Another few steps and she'd be there as well.

Two more steps. One more glance.

Enough.

"What?" she exclaimed, turning and taking a step toward the armed man, realizing too late that he was several inches taller and a heck of a lot broader up close than he'd been with the length of the room between them. But guts and bravado spurred her past the unnerving observation. "Do I have lunch in my teeth? You think I'm some kind of circus sideshow? Why are you staring at me?"

Without batting an eye or missing a beat, he grinned. "You started it."

"I did not." *Snappy, Liza.*

"Holden… We need to walk away." The caution from the detective beside him went unheeded.

Tough Guy faced her, looking as calm and bemused as she was fired up. When a man was armed for battle and built like a fort, he probably didn't feel the need to lose his cool. "Maybe I'm just admiring the view."

Liza scoffed at the flirtatious remark. Right. Like her freckles and attitude had turned his head. "And maybe you're just full of it."

An elbow in the arm from the man standing beside him made the tough guy raise his hands in surrender. "My apologies. Can't help it if I've got a thing for redheads."

"Uh-huh." Liza hadn't expected the apology. Didn't trust it. Wasn't quite sure how to handle it, either.

She nearly jumped out of her skin when she felt a hand at her elbow. She calmed her reaction before it reached her face and looked up into Dr. Jameson's indulgent expression. "Liza? It's not the time for chatting. I want to pursue this while the dream is fresh. Come along."

"Who's chatting?" Liza grumbled. Grateful for the opportunity to escape, she allowed Detective Grove to usher her into a room stuffed with a conference table and chairs. Before the door closed behind her, she gave one last look over her shoulder. The tough guy with the smooth lines and eerily familiar countenance was still watching her. Her reaction to his intense scrutiny was still sparking through her veins. Something about those probing blue eyes was as spellbinding as it was unnerving. Turning away from his inexplicable fascination and determined to dismiss her own, Liza let the door close behind her.

"Who was that man staring at me? I'm sure I've never met him, but he looked… familiar."

Detective Grove glanced toward the door as if her ghost had followed them into the room. "The big guy in the S.W.A.T. vest?" As if anyone else had zeroed in on her through the midday crowd like that. "That's Holden Kincaid."

Liza sank into the nearest chair. "As in Deputy Commissioner John Kincaid?"

"Yeah."

That explained the resemblance. *A thing for redheads, my ass.*

So much for anonymity. If she could figure out who he was, then he had probably identified her as well—the woman who'd reputedly witnessed John Kincaid's murder. Behind that smart-alecky charm, he was probably wondering why the hell she hadn't come forward with the entire story and fingered the killer already.

She'd get right on that. Just as soon as she could remember.

"Holden Kincaid, um…how is he related to the man who was killed?"

Grove spread open the case file at the end of the

table. He could make that bulldog face of his look pretty grim when he wanted to. "He's John's youngest son. And you need to stay away from him."

Chapter Two

"Got him." Holden Kincaid framed the target in the crosshairs of his rifle scope, blinking once to make sure his vision was clear.

Clear like crystal.

His mind and body followed suit, blocking out any distraction that might interfere with the execution of the task at hand. The crisp October air lost its chill. The rough friction of the roofing tiles against the brace of his elbows and thighs vanished. Emotions were put on hold as months of training calmed the beat of his pulse.

Every observation was now made with cold-eyed detachment. From his vantage point atop the neighbor's roof across the alley, he could look right over the privacy fence into Delores Mabry's trashed kitchen. There was a cloudy spot on the window glass, a greasy hand print from the last time the perp had looked out into the back yard. But the smudge didn't mask the gray-haired woman cowering behind a chair against the refrigerator. The window's curtains hung wide open, indicating the target hadn't given much thought to how the police would react to this hostage situation. Holden's target was big enough to make this a relatively easy shot—if his orders had been to shoot to kill.

But as the pudgy stomach in the bright white T-shirt passed by the window again, Holden knew there would be nothing *easy* about this shot.

Al Mabry was armed. He was moving. And the poor SOB probably had no clue to the danger his delusional state had put his mother, himself, and a dozen cops into. Going off his meds did that to a schizophrenic. Mabry was ill. Suicidal. If possible, KCPD wanted to end this standoff with everyone alive. But if Mabry decided to obey the voices in his head and suddenly start shooting up more than the living room furniture, then Holden's orders would change and a life would end.

No emotions allowed.

Static crackled across Holden's helmet radio and Lieutenant Mike Cutler, his S.W.A.T. team leader and scene commander, came online. "You can take that shot?"

Holden rolled his shoulders and neck, easing the last bit of tension from his body before going still in his prone position. "Yes, sir."

"Molloy, can you confirm?"

Dominic Molloy, Holden's lookout, backup and best friend, adjusted his position on the roof beside Holden and peered through his binoculars. "I wouldn't want to take it. But I'm not the big guy." Holden sensed, rather than saw, the teasing grin around the steady chomp of Dom's gum. "The hostage is on the floor," continued Molloy. "Scared out of her mind, maybe, but she doesn't appear to be harmed. Mabry's pacing the kitchen with his gun to his head. Hasn't pointed it at Mama yet. He does lower the weapon when he stops to drink his coffee."

Mabry had ordered his mother to brew a fresh pot earlier. After spending the better part of the past night on this call, Holden longed for some hot coffee himself. Or a hot breakfast. Or a hot… No. He couldn't afford to feel anything right now. *Focus.*

"The perp's routine hasn't varied for the last forty minutes," Holden reported. "The next sip he takes, I could drop him. I think I can even neutralize the gun."

"You think?"

Cutler's skepticism didn't rattle Holden. "Not a problem, sir. My shot is clear."

Dom chuckled beside him. "I see what you're planning." He raised his voice for Cutler and their teammates to hear. "I can confirm. Kincaid can take the shot."

"We've been messin' with this drama long enough," Cutler rumbled. "There's no way to reason with him and I don't want this to escalate." If Mike Cutler couldn't talk a hostage down from his crazy place, then no one could.

Holden was ready to take the next step. "Do you want me to take the shot, sir?"

"Let's get him back in the psych ward. Remember, incapacitate him and we'll take it from there. He hasn't hurt anything but the furniture yet. I'd like to keep it that way." Lieutenant Cutler's tone was concise and commanding—a trait that had always inspired Holden's own confidence. "Assault team ready to move in?"

"Yes, sir." The responses echoed from both the front and rear ground locations.

"You have clearance, Kincaid. Assault team—on my go."

Dom patted the top of Holden's helmet. "You're up, big guy. Do it."

Shoulder? Knee? Either shot would take Mabry

down. Funny how the man who'd murdered Holden's father six months ago had shared the same skills with a gun. One neat shot to the forehead, one to the heart. Clean. Precise. Deadly.

Hell. Where had that thought come from? *Get out of my head.* But the comparison lingered, forcing Holden to think his way through it before he could purge the ill-timed distraction.

The killer had used a hand gun, not a high-powered rifle like the one Holden cradled in his grip. He'd been a good forty yards closer than Holden was to this shot. The victim had been his dad, not a stranger. Had John Kincaid pleaded for his life? Had he held his head high in stoic silence at the end? Had he known death was coming?

Al Mabry didn't know.

Holden's heart quickened with each detail, beating harder against his chest, pumping a familiar rage and sorrow into his veins.

The man who'd killed his father had taken a perverse pleasure in torturing him before pulling the trigger. Holden was a better man than that. Mabry wouldn't die. And if he had to die, he wouldn't suffer. This was his job. Lieutenant Cutler's S.W.A.T. team was here to save the damn day.

"Get out of my head," he muttered, willing his training to retake control of his emotions.

"What's that, buddy?" Dom asked.

This is my job.

"Taking the shot." Holden iced his nerves, stilled his breath, framed the target in his sights and squeezed the trigger.

Boom.

Holden's shoulder absorbed the kick of the rifle. Glass shattered and Al Mabry screamed.

"Go!" Cutler's order echoed through his helmet.

Crimson bloomed on the perp's hand as the gun sailed across the kitchen. Holden quickly lined up a second shot to the perp's left temple in case things went south. But before Al Mabry could fully understand that he'd been shot, Holden's teammates had battered down the door and rushed the mentally disturbed young man. Jones and Delgado had Mabry facedown on the floor with his hands cuffed behind his back, the gun secured, before Holden allowed himself another blink.

The hate and sorrow were buried. The ice remained. Closing his eyes, Holden finally allowed himself to breathe.

"All clear, big guy." Dom sat up beside him. His boots grated on the gravel roof as he stowed his gear into the various compartments of his uniform. With the flat of his hand, he reached over and slapped Holden's helmet. "Hey. Cutler gave us the 'all clear.' I guess there's a reason why they call you the best. You *were* aiming for the gun, right?"

Even more than the chatter of commands and replies zinging from the radio in his helmet, Dom's gibe reminded Holden that he needed to get moving.

Striving for the same detachment from his work that Dominic Molloy seemed to enjoy, Holden rolled over, splayed his hand in Molloy's face and pushed him away. He could give as good as he got. "Jealous, much?"

"You wish." Dom's eyes sparkled with humor. "I could have made that shot if I wanted to. But it's my job to watch your backside."

Holden secured his rifle and picked up the tripod as he pushed to his feet and made his way toward the ladder at the front edge of the roof. "Then enjoy the view. Last man down buys the beer."

Once on the ground, they shed their helmets and locked their equipment in the back of the black S.W.A.T. van. Combing his fingers through the sweat-dampened spikes of his hair, Holden crossed down to the street to join Rafael Delgado and Joseph Jones, Jr.—Triple J or Trip, as he liked to be called.

He held up his hand to urge the gathering crowd of curiosity-seekers off the street while the others guided the ambulance carrying Al Mabry through. Lieutenant Cutler followed right behind, signaling the EMTs when they were clear to take off. Cutler joined the team as they gathered at the van. The lieutenant congratulated them on a successful mission, reminded them to write their reports. Then he shook Holden's hand and pulled him aside. "Nice shooting, Kincaid."

The October morning had enough bite in it to create a cloud between them when Holden released a long, weary breath. Winter was going to be damp and cold—and early—this year in Kansas City. "Thanks, Lieutenant."

"We'll get Mabry to the hospital to stitch up his hand and have him evaluated. But he'll be all right."

Holden propped his hands at his hips and nodded toward the house. "Take his mother, too. You said she had a history of high blood pressure. Being taken hostage by her own son can't be good for her health."

"Don't worry. She's on the ambulance, too. We'll let her decompress, then take her statement at the hospital. I want you to do the same."

"Go to the hospital?" Other than being hungry as a bear and needing to take a whiz, Holden was in fine shape.

"Decompress. You're wound up tighter than a cork in a champagne bottle. You've been on duty twenty-four hours, standing watch while we tried to talk Mabry off the ceiling for the last eight." Cutler pulled off his KCPD ball cap and smoothed his hand over his salt-and-pepper hair before tugging the cap back into place. "Your dad would be proud of you today. By wounding Al Mabry, you probably saved his life. And his mother's. He was an innocent man, a sick man, but I know you were prepared to make a kill shot."

"Just doing my job, Lieutenant. I turn off thinking about anything," he lied, "and take the shot you tell me to."

"Uh-huh." There was something in Cutler's sharp, dark eyes that saw more than Holden wanted. So he scuffed the steel toe of his boot on the pavement and looked down to watch a tiny pebble fly against the curb—until Cutler's words demanded his attention. "Think about this, Kincaid. Before you report for your next shift, I want to hear that you got drunk, got laid or got checked out by the departmental psychologist. I know this has been a tough year for you, and this was a tough scene to work. Go home. Go out. Go to the doc. But take care of yourself."

"Yes, sir."

Dominic materialized at Holden's shoulder, his wise-ass grin firmly in place. "Aren't you gonna order me to go get some tail, too, sir?"

"That'd just be feeding the fire."

Trip and Delgado joined the circle, laughing out loud at Cutler's deadpan reply.

"Ha. Ha." Dom slapped Holden on the shoulder. "C'mon, big guy. We'll check out the action at the Shamrock after we clean up and get a bite to eat. Drinks are on me." He turned to Trip and Delgado. "You comin'?"

"You're gonna pry open that tight wallet of yours?" Trip's lazy drawl mocked him with awestruck humor. "This I gotta see."

"Lieutenant?" Dom looked up at their commander. "You're welcome to join us."

"I'll pass this time. My son has a football game tonight. I'll check in with you guys day after tomorrow. Don't forget those reports."

A chorus of "yes, sir's" quickly changed into a noisy conversation about the new lady bartender at the Shamrock and whether she had any sisters she'd like to introduce to them. Delgado climbed in behind the wheel and started the van while the rest of the team buckled themselves in. Holden had found the woman pretty enough the last time they'd gone to the Shamrock, but for some reason he was having a hard time remembering what she looked like.

He must be off his game big time, to let his feelings about his father's murder distract him from his work—and his play time—and to let them distract him enough that Lieutenant Cutler had noticed.

He'd been through all the grief counseling, and had been cleared by the department's psychologist to return to duty four months ago. He hadn't lied to Cutler or the psychologist about his and his three brothers' determination to see their father's killer brought to justice. Even though they weren't allowed to work the case because of a conflict of interest, Holden, Atticus, Sawyer and Edward had all found ways to keep tabs on the stalled-out investigation.

Atticus and his fiancée, Brooke Hansford, had uncovered evidence about a covert organization named Z Group that had operated in eastern Europe before the breakup of the Soviet Union. Before becoming a cop at KCPD, their father had worked with Brooke's late parents in Z Group as a liaison from Army intelligence. Something that had happened to a double agent all those years ago in a foreign country had gotten John Kincaid killed.

His brother Sawyer and his pregnant wife, Melissa, had dealt with an offshoot of Z Group soon after their father's funeral. But one of the thugs hired by the group had had a personal vendetta against Melissa. He'd terrorized her and kidnapped their young son. Despite the opportunity to blow open the murder investigation, Sawyer had done what any husband would have—he protected his family. John Kincaid would have done the same—any of Holden's brothers would have—so there was no blame there. Now, Melissa and their child were safe, but anyone who could tell them anything had been driven into hiding or killed.

And yesterday morning, while Atticus had been reporting on the trip he and Brooke had taken to Sarajevo to visit her parents' graves—only to discover that it wasn't her mother's body that had been buried in that casket nearly thirty years ago—Holden had run smack dab into Liza Parrish. A name he wasn't supposed to know. A woman he wasn't supposed to meet.

The lone witness to his father's murder.

Yeah. He was a little distracted.

A lot distracted.

Liza Parrish could make the scattered pieces of this whole jigsaw puzzle fall into place. His father's killer would be brought to trial and the Kincaid family could finally find peace.

So why wasn't she talking? Why wasn't she telling the detectives assigned to the investigation everything she knew?

And why the hell couldn't he remember what the sexy bartender looked like, the one who'd slipped him her number at the Shamrock, when he had no trouble whatsoever picturing freckles and copper hair, a sweet, round bottom and an attitude that wouldn't quit?

As much as his father's murder challenged his ability to focus on his work, little Miss Liza with the sass and curves—and answers—kept nagging at him like an itch he couldn't scratch. If he couldn't get his head together, he'd be a bigger danger to his team than the bad guys they were trained to neutralize.

Cutler realized that.

"Yo, big guy." Dom smacked him on the shoulder, pulling Holden from his thoughts. "I said whoever got Josie's number first would have to buy the second round of drinks tonight. You in?"

Josie. Right. That was the bartender's name. Yet it was hard to razz his buddies about the fact he already had her number, when he couldn't even recall the color of her hair.

But copper-red? Short—almost boyishly cropped and sexy as hell? *That* he could remember.

He was so screwed. Faking a lightheartedness he didn't feel, Holden fixed a grin on his face and turned to Dom. "You're on."

It was a hollow victory. But right now he'd take whatever victory he could get.

HOLDEN'S LONG STRIDES ATE UP the pavement as he ran the abandoned Union Pacific railroad bed. It had been reclaimed as part of an exercise trail along Rock Creek, near the Kansas City suburb of Fairmount, and would make for a scenic run in the daylight, with the red, gold and orange leaves of the old maples and oaks rising along the hills to his left and flattening out to the residential streets to his right.

Pulling back the cuff of his sweatshirt, he pushed the button for light on his watch and checked the time. At 11:27 p.m., however, the deserted path was gray and shadowed beneath the cool moonlight. Still, it was a good place to get away from the traffic and crowd near his downtown apartment without venturing too far from the amenities of the city.

Hanging out with his buddies at the Shamrock hadn't provided the cure Lieutenant Cutler had prescribed. Al Mabry was fine and full of remorse now that he was back with his doctors at the Odd Fellows Psychiatric Hospital. His mother, Delores, was resting comfortably at Truman Medical Center for a night of routine observation. No one had been seriously hurt. Holden had made a good shot. They should all be celebrating.

But the beer and noise had given him a headache. The greasy food had been tasty enough, but it had sat like a rock in his stomach. As for the women? Well, when doing a little flirting began to feel like a polite chore he had to perform, Holden knew he needed to get out of there.

With the honest excuse of a long day and a longer night before that dragging him down, he shook Dominic's hand, warned Delgado and Trip to keep an eye on him, and left. Instead of heading home, though, he found himself at his Fourth Precinct police locker, changing into his gray sweats and running shoes. After a brief chat with his brother, Atticus, who was there to pick up Brooke for a late dinner after a meeting with her boss, precinct commander Mitch Taylor, Holden pulled on his black KCPD stocking cap and headed across town.

Sleep might have been a wiser choice, but Holden was more inclined to get his blood and adrenaline pumping, and cleanse himself of this restless apprehension from the inside out.

Normally, he was content to work out in the precinct's gym or run the streets near his apartment. But tonight, he needed something fresh and different to shake him out of this funk. The brisk dampness in the air would clear his head, while every turn on the route would reveal something new to pique his interest.

And if the path just happened to lead him past the address where Liza Parrish lived, then that could be excused as coincidence. The houses were close to the road, but set far enough apart to almost give the feeling of living out in the country. Probably at one time in Kansas City's history, this had been farmland, but with expansion and annexations, the neighborhood was inevitably being transformed into suburbia. As he passed a quarter mile of grass and trees, he realized how this must seem like a different world from the downtown animal clinic where Liza worked an internship through the University of Missouri College of Veterinary Medicine.

"Are you looking up what I think you are?" Atticus had caught Holden sitting at a computer in one of the darkened precinct offices. Leading his fiancée by the hand, he'd entered the room before Holden was even aware of his presence.

Brooke peeked around Atticus's shoulder with a wry smile. "Sorry. We were on our way to the car when I mentioned that I'd seen you here. He figured out the rest."

His smarty-pants older brother never missed a trick, so there was no sense in lying to him. Holden folded the print-out he'd made and shut down the computer. "Yeah. I checked out the public information available on Liza Parrish. Brooke just told me where to find it on the computer."

"You helped him?" Shaking his head, Atticus turned to Brooke. "Honey, we talked about this. As much as it galls me to sit on the sidelines, we have to let Grove and his men run their investigation."

Brooke adjusted her glasses on her nose and softened her expression into a smile that always seemed to turn his brother's suave control into mush. "That's not what you said this summer, when we were on a hunt to decipher the clues your father left me. You were certainly involved in the investigation then."

"Yeah, well, we both know what kind of danger that 'investigation' put you in. I don't want to see anyone else get hurt."

She lay a calming hand on Atticus's arm. "All I did was show Holden a shortcut to the public access files on the computer. So he wouldn't accidentally trigger any security protocol that might alert Grove or anyone else to his search."

Holden circled around the desk and draped an arm around her shoulders. "I knew if I had a computer question, Brooke was the source to go to. I didn't mean to get her into trouble."

As their father's former secretary, Brooke had been a friend for so long that she felt like family. Holden had been more than pleased to see that Atticus had opened up his heart and put an engagement ring on her finger to make that familial feeling into the real thing. So he wasn't about to let his leggy buddy here accept any of his brother's blame.

But Atticus wasn't angry, nor was he looking to place blame. His pale gray eyes reflected concern and an ad-

miration for Brooke's talents that went far beyond her computer skills.

"Brains as well as beauty, eh?" He pulled Brooke from Holden's hug and curled her under his possessive arm. After pressing a kiss to Brooke's temple, Atticus gave Holden a look as serious as any he'd ever seen. "Just be careful, little brother. Don't get caught sticking your nose where it doesn't belong." He guided Brooke to the door, then paused to glance over his shoulder. "And if you find out anything, give me a call."

Holden grinned. Yeah, Mr. Serious was not only crazy in love but as determined as he was to find the whole truth about their father's murder. "Will do."

So now he was here with his brother's blessing, running his third mile, wondering why the hell he'd thought checking out Liza Parrish's place would give him any sense of peace. He was working up a sweat and getting irritated with himself because no matter how hard he pushed his body, his thoughts kept coming back to the freckle-faced witness who could make or break the investigation.

At least Holden wasn't as alone in this misguided late night jaunt as he'd first thought. Someone else was out on foot, either walking the streets a couple blocks over or biking or running the path ahead of him, closer to the houses. One by one, he could hear dogs barking at the intruder passing their territory.

Holden's senses pricked up a notch to a mild alert. This wasn't a dangerous part of town, but it was pretty remote for a woman who lived alone to reside in. Surely, Liza Parrish wouldn't be out for a stroll at this time of night. The woman did possess some common sense, didn't she? Of course, her preliminary deposition to

KCPD said she'd been chasing after a stray near the docks in the warehouse district where his father had been murdered. Late at night. And that was definitely a dangerous part of town. Maybe he should hold off on the common sense assessment until…

Another bark pierced the night, turning his attention back to the houses. It was something yippy, aggressive, much closer than the other sounds had been. Holden's wariness sharpened the way it did when a call came in for the S.W.A.T. team. Maybe it'd be worth a detour through one of the yards to the nearest street to find out what was putting all those mutts on alert.

Lengthening his stride, Holden veered toward the next access point and rounded the corner, straight into the path of a fast-moving pack. "Ah, hell!"

The woman holding on to that pack gave a curse as pithy as his own, a fact which amused him for all of two seconds before he realized she was zigging when she should have zagged. Between his bulk, the momentum of the three dogs, the tangle of leashes and the speed of her roller blades, the collision was inevitable.

"Look out!" Holden threw his arms out to catch her.

The smallest of the dogs darted between his legs. The greyhound leaped and the big malamute just kept running.

"Yukon!" the woman shouted as her helmet smacked into Holden's shoulder.

Recognition was as surprising as it was irrelevant. A leash jerked around Holden's ankles, cinching his legs and abruptly tripping his feet. "Hold on!"

He snaked his arms around the redhead's waist and twisted, dodging the dogs and taking the brunt of their fall as they went down hard. Holden landed on his back with Liza Parrish sprawled across his chest.

"What the hell…? You?" Liza froze above him. The sounds of panting dogs and her accusation filled the air. Her eyes caught the moonlight and reflected like silver coins. But there was more fire than cold metal in their expression as surprise quickly changed into indignation. Bracing one fist against his shoulder, she pushed herself up. "Are you following me?"

"I… damn." Holden sat up as best he could with a nylon lead looped around his neck as she clambered backward onto his thighs. He loosened the cord and pulled it over his head. "I ran *into* you, Sherlock—I didn't run up behind you. Nobody's following anybody. Watch it," he added as a skate came dangerously close to the promised land in her struggle to extricate herself from his lap. "Ow!" That was because of the malamute, still eager to run, dragging them both off the curb.

"Yukon, no! Stop! Catch his leash!" Liza had lost her grip on the leads in their tumble, and the biggest dog took a shot at freedom.

Holden lunged for the disappearing strap. "Got it." The big dog nearly pulled Holden's arm from its socket, but Holden tugged back. "Whoa!" With the sudden jerk on his lead, the gray and white malamute halted, turned. His dark, nearly black eyes seemed to tell Holden exactly what he could do with his command. "Is he friendly?"

"Not much."

Great, thought Holden. "Yukon. Sit." The malamute needed a minute to think about it.

"Sit!" Holden gave the leash a slight jerk. He was feeling bruised and off-kilter and slightly less amused by this situation than he might have been on any normal day with any other woman sitting in his lap.

The dog shook his silver fur, then curled his bushy tail around his backside and eased back onto his haunches.

"Sorry." The fringe of Liza's coppery hair was barely visible beneath the rim of her helmet as she adjusted it on her head. Then she slid onto her kneepads beside him and tried to untangle the leashes that bound their legs together. "He doesn't warm up to people easily, but as far as I know, he doesn't bite. Bruiser's the one who'll nip—"

A miniature German Shepherd-looking terrier thing jumped, barking, onto Holden's thigh and stretched as close to Holden's face as his ensnared leash allowed. He recognized the yipping bark from earlier. "Um…"

"Bruiser. Sit." Liza snapped her fingers and pointed, and the black and tan spitfire moved back to the pavement and obeyed.

"Sweet." He admired her authority over the dog. Not counting the tan greyhound who was sniffing his stocking cap, the canines seemed to be under control. Holden joined the quest to untangle themselves, but a closer inspection revealed the pale cast beneath the freckles on Liza's cheeks. "Are you hurt?"

She shook her head. "That's what the helmet and pads are for." She spun around on her knees to untangle the red leash that had wound around his ankles. "Are you?"

"I'm fine." In fact, he barely noticed the ache in his shoulder and hip. Sheathed in fitted black running pants, her firmly rounded bottom bounced in front of him. Holden politely looked away—for a second or two. Heck, he was a healthy young male, and she was definitely a healthy young female. *Holden Kincaid.* He shifted uncomfortably as his mother's voice reminded him of her expectations about how a lady should be treated. Ogling wasn't on the list. Ignoring the improper heat simmering in his veins, Holden turned his attention to the greyhound who insisted on being petted. He stroked her smooth, warm flank. "I guess the dogs are okay, too? Are these guys all yours?"

Liza glanced up long enough to visually inspect each creature. "I'm sure they're fine." She continued to work quickly, almost frantically, to extricate herself and the dogs. When Holden reached down to help, she snatched her fingers away to attack a different tangle.

In another few moments they were free. Holden pulled his feet beneath him and stood while she looped the handle of each leash around her wrist. He took her arm to help her stand. But as soon as she was upright, she shrugged off his touch, nearly toppling herself again. "Easy," he murmured.

She skated backward far enough to put her beyond his well-intentioned reach. When she was firmly balanced on her wheels, she tilted her chin and glared. Her puff of breath clouded the air between them. "What are you doing here? I'm not supposed to be talking to you."

"Well, it's a little late for that." But she clearly wasn't one for sarcasm, so he turned to more serious matters, and gestured up and down the empty path. "You should find an indoor track if you want to run at night."

She pulled the dogs between them and straightened their leads. "And who would allow these three to join me? They need their exercise, too."

"Then how about running in the daylight? Even with the dogs to protect you—" not that the greyhound nuzzling his hand was any great deterrent, "—this path is isolated enough to make it a dangerous place to run at night."

"You're here," she argued.

"It takes a few more guts to go after someone my size

than yours." She was above-average height, and the wheels on her skates put her at eye-level with his chin. But there was still something distinctly feminine and vulnerable about her slender curves and youthful freckles that could catch a determined predator's eye. "Any woman should take the proper precautions."

Her eyes darted to the side as she seemed to consider his advice. But there was nothing but bold bravado in her expression when she tipped her chin to meet his gaze again. "You're John Kincaid's son. Do you know who I am?"

"Yeah." There was no sense lying about what she must have already guessed. "I'm Holden Kincaid and you're Liza Parrish." He extended his hand to complete the introduction.

She didn't take it. Instead, she wound the three leashes around her palm and tested their snug fit. "You're not here by accident, are you. Detective Grove and the D.A. want to keep my face and name out of the papers—keep me as anonymous as possible. How did you find me?"

"I'm a cop."

"You shouldn't be here. I shouldn't be talking to you."

"So you keep saying." Propping his hands at his hips, Holden leaned in a fraction. "But my brothers and I intend to find out the truth about what happened to our father. A gag order isn't going to keep us from knowing that you're the key witness. What story are you telling Grove? Did you see who killed my father?"

"I can't answer those questions."

Maybe assertive cop mode wasn't the best approach here. He reached down and scratched behind the ears of the willing greyhound, suspecting the dogs might be the way to gain her trust. "What's her name?"

"Cruiser." The confident voice hesitated, as though suspicious of the new tactic. "She's a rescue hound. She used to race. They're all rescue dogs. The little guy's Bruiser and the big guy is Yukon."

Though the terrier mix seemed to be watching the interchange between mistress and stranger intently, the malamute faced away from them, looking poised and eager to continue their run. Holden said, "I know it's scary to come forward to work with the police, especially when there's a murder involved. But we have teams in place who can protect you. KCPD and the D.A.'s office won't let anyone hurt you. Just tell Grove the truth. He'll make the arrangements to put you in a safe house if you're worried about some kind of retaliation." He looked up from petting his new friend and offered Liza a gentle plea. "This case has been dragging on forever. The longer it takes to solve it, the less likely it is that we will."

The conversation seemed to rattle her independent attitude. Her silvery gaze blinked, fell to his chest, wandered off into the shadows. The abrasive woman who'd avoided his touch and given him lip was now avoiding eye contact and backing away. "I really can't help you. I mean, I want to, but—I don't think I can help you."

"You don't have to break protocol and talk to me," Holden reassured her, "but please be completely honest with Detective Grove. Tomorrow. As soon as you can."

"I need to be going." She turned away, clicked her tongue at the dogs. "Good night, Mr. Kincaid."

"It's Holden." But she was already skating ahead with her dogs, crouching slightly and holding on as the two bigger dogs pulled her down the path. Little Bruiser jogged along behind. In less than a minute she was out of sight beyond the trees and shadows.

Holden tipped his face to the moon, cursing his dumb luck and dumber idea for coming here in the first place. So he'd said his piece to Liza Parrish—gotten that much frustration out of his system. Instead of speeding the process, he'd probably terrorized the woman into being even more afraid of sharing everything she knew with the police.

He took a few moments to stretch before resuming his run. A few moments to realize that her scent clung to his shirt, citrusy and fresh, with a tinge of antiseptic thrown in. Feminine. Clean. It only intensified his improper fascination with the woman.

He gave himself a mocking thumbs-up. "Way to get her out of your head, Kincaid."

He'd better make that appointment with the department shrink because he didn't feel like getting drunk and when he was off his clear-headed game like this, he had no business getting laid.

Looking around the maze of shadows and moonlight, Holden forced himself to think like a cop. Things had quieted down in the neighborhood now that Liza and her pack had passed through. But the exercise path was still deserted. It was still nearly midnight. Even if she wasn't a murder witness, this wasn't the safest route for a lone woman to take.

Holden inhaled a deep breath and turned around. Keeping his distance so she didn't know he was following, he jogged after Liza and her dogs, keeping a watchful eye out. That's all his family needed—to have something freaky happen to the eccentric, albeit finely built, redhead who could identify his father's killer.

Chapter Three

"Bruiser, you mooch—get your nose off the counter. Brownies aren't for dogs." Without pausing to let Liza remove his leash, her furry soul mate had trotted straight into the kitchen to inspect the pan she'd left out on the counter to cool. Liza locked the door behind her and sat on the Hide-a-bench in the front hallway to remove her skates. "Besides, they're mine."

Chocolate was a good antidote for a stressful day, and she'd been craving the sweet stuff more than usual lately. If she thought Bruiser's short legs could handle it, she'd add another mile to their nightly run to make up for the indulgence. As it was, she'd better watch how many "antidotes" she baked after dinner or the stress would start to show on her hips.

But she'd start watching tomorrow. After the week she'd been having—too little sleep, too much work, therapy sessions that left her agitated, embarrassed and more uncertain than ever that she could recall anything useful about John Kincaid's murder, plus two run-ins with John's overbuilt, in-her-face and under-her-skin son—she deserved a double-sized brownie tonight.

Liza lifted the top of the bench seat and dropped her

inline skates, helmet and pads into the storage compartment inside. She finger-combed her hair back into its wispy layers and whistled for the dogs. Bruiser and Cruiser showed up right away to let her unhook their leashes and reward them with a treat. "I'm feeding myself first, Yukon, if you don't come when I call you." She whistled again. "Here, boy. Yukon, come."

He barely acknowledged her from his spot on the couch.

"Fine. We're eating without you." She padded to the kitchen in her stockinged feet, shedding her jacket and hanging it over the back of a kitchen chair as she went. Then she opened a cabinet and reached for a plate to serve herself a brownie. "Ouch."

Drawing her arm back for a closer inspection, Liza cradled her elbow and slowly twisted it from side to side. How could she have missed hurting herself? She must have jarred her funny bone pretty good in her tumble with Kincaid. Though she'd like to credit the endorphins released during that final mile of her run for masking the injury, she had a feeling her preoccupation with Officer Kincaid was the real culprit that had kept her from feeling any pain until now.

How embarrassing, crashing into a man she wasn't even supposed to meet. Pressing her body against his from chest to toe. Noticing things.

Even in those few short moments they were tangled together on the pavement, she'd noticed he was A) incredibly warm, despite the temperature's drop into the 30s; B) built like an Olympic swimmer—long and solid and packed with muscle, hinting that he probably enjoyed sports and working out as much as she did; and C) he had the most beautiful eyelashes she'd ever seen on a man. Light brown, long and framing piercing blue eyes.

"Stop it." Liza chomped a bit of brownie that was too big for her mouth, determined to take note of every sweet, chewy detail of her snack rather than wasting another moment thinking about Holden Kincaid. "He's just a man," she muttered around the mouthful.

A man who happened to bear a discomfiting resemblance to the murder victim who haunted her dreams.

"Yeah. There's no bad omen about that, is there." She swallowed her sarcasm along with her brownie. "C'mon, guys."

After tossing a couple of rawhide chews down to Bruiser and Cruiser, and tucking one into Yukon's dish, Liza poured herself a glass of milk. With the glass in one hand and a plate of chocolate therapy in the other, she joined the dogs in the living room. She didn't bother turning on a light or picking up the remote. There wasn't much on TV she wanted to watch at this time of night, and sitting with her three best friends—make that two friends and a maybe, as Yukon hopped down when she tried to join him on the couch—would help her unwind so that she'd have a shot at five or six hours of uninterrupted sleep.

Yukon ambled off to the kitchen to enjoy his rawhide in solitude while Cruiser curled up on the cushion beside Liza and Bruiser stretched out at her feet. The quiet was soothing, her body replete from exercise and fresh air. Once the initial sugar rush wore off, the chocolate and milk and late night should make her sleepy.

With her eyes adjusted to the interior darkness, she could see the sparse practicality of her furnishings. One woman didn't need a lot, especially when she spent the majority of her time at work or in class. And with three dogs of her own, and others she fostered from time to time living here, she didn't want a lot of good furniture around that could be turned into dog beds, or a house filled with sentimental knickknacks that might be accidentally broken by a wagging tail.

Still, the darkness revealed the loneliness of her existence. She'd put most of her parents' belongings into storage after their deaths—or had given them away to relatives and charities. As a college student, she'd lived in a small apartment with no space for such things, but mainly, as an orphaned nineteen-year-old, she hadn't wanted reminders of all that had been taken from her.

The one family photo she kept on her bookshelf looked mighty lonely. Maybe after six years, she was ready to face her past on a day-to-day basis without breaking into tears or clenching her fists in anger. She should unpack one of the embroidered pillows her mother had made, or put one of her father's bowling trophies out beside the photo so that the picture wouldn't seem so lonesome. So that *she* wouldn't feel so lonesome.

Almost as if she could read her thoughts, Cruiser nudged her head into Liza's lap and demanded she be petted. Liza smiled and obliged, smoothing her hand along the graying muzzle and stroking the dog's streamlined head. "How can I be lonely with you guys here?"

Talking to dogs and missing her parents—yeah, the darkness revealed an awful lot.

Including the tall black SUV parked across the street.

A faint blip of awareness nudged its way into Liza's brain. "What the…?"

Suddenly, the stench of garbage and an icy dampness

chilling her skin were as real to her as they'd been on that April night down by the Missouri River when two gunshots had rent the air. Almost as if she was plunging down into a black hole, reality deserted her and she found herself alone in a dark alley, with only fear and death and a starving dog for company. Everything around her was black—the wall in front of her. No, not a wall. A car. A big black—

Bruiser's high-pitched bark yanked her firmly back into the reality of the late October night. Cruiser jumped off the couch and joined the smaller dog at the front window, offering a token bark of her own. A delivery-man coming to the door was usually the only thing that got them this excited.

"Hush, you two," Liza chided as she climbed to her feet. "You'll wake the neighbors."

Yukon beat her to the window to check out the commotion. Pushing aside the dog and pulling back the sheer curtain, Liza peered out at the vehicle. Any shiver of unease was overshadowed by the three-dog alarm going off in her house. Wait a minute. Was that…? Her gaze zeroed in on the oversized man sitting behind the wheel. Surely he wouldn't…

Liza's nerve endings hummed with awareness, waking her senses. She leaned forward. There were a million black cars in the world. Nothing particularly profound about this one except… There was definitely someone in that car. Not her neighbor's car. Not her neighbor. "Oh, my God."

The shadows beyond the circle of light cast by the nearest streetlamp kept her from making out a face. But the bulk of the man's shoulders looked familiar. There was no exhaust coming from the back of the car, so the engine wasn't running. He was just sitting there. Watching. Big man. Too close. Paying too much attention to her and her house.

"The nerve of that guy." She was already striding toward the front door. "Just leave me alone, already."

Trusting her temper would keep her warm, and that telling off the nosy cop wouldn't take two seconds, Liza unlocked the door and stepped outside. The moisture collecting on the concrete of her front step soaked into her socks but didn't stop her.

"Hey! Kincaid!" She marched down the sidewalk, pointing her finger at the tinted glass and silhouetted driver inside. "For the last time, quit following me. You know damn well we're not supposed to have contact. You're going to get yourself in trouble." She reached the street and angled her approach, heading straight for the car. "Besides, you've got my dogs all fired up and I don't want a complaint—"

All of a sudden, the headlights came on, flashing the high beams into her eyes. "Hey! Damn it, Kincaid!"

She threw her arms up in front of her face, shielding her eyes. The next curse out of her mouth died when she heard the engine turn over and rev up on all cylinders. "Kincaid…?"

The grinding pitch of rubber tires spinning against asphalt screeched in her ears.

Not good.

By the time the tires found traction, Liza was already running, diving toward the curb as the SUV barreled toward her. She hit the grass and slid, feeling the wind of the speeding car whip past her, and the cold muck of the damp ground seeping into her clothes.

"You son of a bitch." That was no accident. He had

to have seen her. He was a cop, for Pete's sake. Whatever happened to "serve and protect"? Liza pushed up on her hands and knees. "Kincaid!" She stood as the SUV spun around the corner, kicking up gravel and speeding out of sight. "You son of a—"

"Liza!"

Footsteps pounded the pavement behind her. A hand grabbed her arm. She yelped, spun around. Saw a ghost.

"Are you hurt?"

She shook her head, squeezing her eyes shut against the ball bearings rolling around inside her skull. "How did you…?"

"You okay?" She blinked her eyes open. Kincaid was still there. Tall. Broad. Close. He glanced over the top of her head, then behind him, looking in every direction before zeroing in on her. "I saw that idiot peel out of here. Not that you're a whole lot smarter for running out in front of him—"

"I don't understand…." The ground rushed up beneath her.

"You're *not* okay."

Strong arms caught her as she sank to the curb. Long fingers pushed her head forward between her knees, and massaged the back of her neck until the faintness passed.

As Liza regained her senses, the dark asphalt dusted with bits of gravel came into focus. She became aware of the warmth springing from her neck and circulating out into her stiff limbs. She marveled at the size of the big running shoe lined up beside her narrower, muddy sock.

She was sitting outside on a damp autumn night next to Holden Kincaid. And she was squeezing his big, sturdy hand between hers as though it was the only lifeline to keep her from drowning in a swirling pool of nightmares.

The comfort she should have taken from that hand ended as soon as the realization was made.

"Remember!"

Suddenly, in her mind's eye, she was clutching a bony corpse's hand. The touch was cold and dead, not warm and full of life. *"Remember."*

Liza jerked her hand away. "If only I could," she murmured, rubbing away at the imagined chill that remained.

"If only you could what?"

Why was she so certain she'd recognized that big man? That stranger? She didn't know him. Didn't know that car. Didn't know enough about anything anymore to properly protect herself.

The massage at her nape went still. "Liza. Talk to me. What just happened?"

Even at a whisper, the timbre of his voice was deep and resonant, and utterly soothing.

She pointed her thumb toward the intersection where the SUV had turned. "I thought you were stalking me."

"What?"

"I was so certain that was you." Liza lifted her chin and looked Holden in the eye. She touched her fingertips to the prickly stubble shading his jaw, reassuring herself that he was real. That he was here. That she wasn't crazy. The heat of remorse warmed her cheeks and she curled her fingers into her palm. He was real enough, and she'd been completely unfair to be so suspicious of his intentions. "I'm sorry."

"Besides the fact that I drive a red Mustang parked

three miles from here, I'm not in the habit of running down women in the middle of the street."

"Only on the exercise path."

A slow smile eased the grave intensity from his face. "Good one. But, for the record, you and your pack ran into me."

She felt herself smiling back. "We tend to go wherever Yukon wants."

"I can imagine."

Liza shivered. She hugged her arms across her middle, unsure whether the chill came from the cold seeping in through her soggy clothes or her mind recalling just how close she'd come to being roadkill. "Why would someone do that? Was that road rage for yelling at him?"

"I got a plate number, so I'll call it in, see if we can pick him up." Holden stood, towering over her huddled position. "Could be nothing personal at all, just a dangerous drunk who shouldn't be behind the wheel tonight. I'll take care of it."

He'd take care of it? What? No. She handled her problems her own self. That was just the way she operated. Still, the concise, confident words were reassuring, even if spoken by this Montague she wasn't supposed to be talking to. "Thank you."

"Can you stand?"

Liza nodded. When he reached down to take her hand, she avoided it and the disturbing nightmare his tight grip conjured, drawing herself up onto her own two feet. But when he flattened his palm at the small of her back, checking up and down the street before escorting her across, Liza didn't pull away.

She'd grown halfway accustomed to his casual yet protective touch by the time they reached her front door.

But as guilty as she felt about believing he'd purposely meant to harass or hurt her, she wasn't prepared to invite him inside to make amends.

"Why are you still here?"

He pointed to his chest. "Cop, remember? Besides, my mom says I should always walk the lady to her door, no matter what the night was like."

"If tonight was a date, it'd rank as pretty lousy, wouldn't it?"

"It wouldn't have been all bad. I mean, considering neither one of us had to be rushed to the hospital...."

She laughed before she could stop herself, but quickly fell silent. After all, this *wasn't* a date. "I meant, why are you even at my house? In my neighborhood? We parted ways twenty minutes ago."

He nodded, shifting his supporting hand to her arm to guide her up onto the front step before releasing her. "I ran to the end of the path and was on my way back when I heard somebody cursing my name. Pretty loudly, I might add."

Liza cringed before turning around to face him. "Sorry about that. I saw the big silhouette of a man in the car, remembered how you were watching me at the police station yesterday—"

"I told you I was admiring the view."

Standing on the step above him, her eyes looked straight into his. She couldn't tell if the dark blue irises were being mischievous or sincere, but she could say that either possibility intrigued her. "Right. You have a thing for redheads. I still don't believe that line."

Definitely mischievous. "Why were you staring at *me?*"

Because you remind me of a dead guy?

That sobering thought put the brakes on the inexplicable desire to continue sparring with the man. She wasn't so starved for human interaction or rattled by nearly getting run over that she'd let her sarcasm go to that place. "You remind me of…" *Your father.* What was she doing? Inhaling a deep, cleansing breath, Liza fixed the coolest, most reserved expression she could muster onto her face. "You remind me of someone I met once. Thanks for your help, but this is awkward. Detective Grove said I shouldn't have contact with your family, in case this goes to trial and I have to testify—"

"This *will* go to trial." His friendly, amused expression disappeared behind a mask that was all cop, all man, all business—and frankly, a little scary. "Anything you can do to help Grove find Dad's killer, and build the case against him—I *need* you to do that. My brothers and mom—and me, too—we need your help. Please tell Grove exactly what you saw so that we can move on this investigation. If you're afraid of some kind of retribution from the killer, KCPD has safe-houses. We can protect you."

So that was why he was here. Why he'd picked her out of the crowd and watched her at the police station. Why he was being charming and attentive now. Why he was ignoring Detective Grove's recommendation and having this face-to-face conversation with her.

Save the day. Name the killer. Fix their broken lives. No pressure. No guilt.

The chocolate brownie burned like acid in her stomach. No memory? No damn way she could help him.

Liza withdrew, both literally and figuratively, reaching behind her for the doorknob. "I'd better go in, and get into a hot shower before all these bumps and bruises take hold. I'm sorry I thought that driver was you. I know you're one of the good guys."

"Please, Liza." He stepped forward, she backed away. Understanding his pain and frustration, she tried to summon an apologetic smile, but failed. "I'm so sorry for your loss. Good night, Kincaid."

His hands fisted at his sides, and the effort it took to hold himself still and stop pushing the issue emanated from him in waves. "Good night, Parrish."

She stood there in the open doorway, clutching the knob behind her, wanting to reach out to the sorrow tempered by confusion etched on his face. Wanting to say something, but fairly certain that nothing she could explain about amnesia or her own losses or good intentions would give him comfort.

He must have misread her silence. "I'm not moving until I hear you lock the door on the other side."

"Oh." Embarrassed that she couldn't seem to separate what she *should* do from what that lonely nugget of need inside her *wanted* to do, Liza turned and went inside, closing the door behind her and bolting it. There was no sense prolonging their goodbyes or wanting anything besides to be left alone.

Suddenly drained of energy, Liza leaned against the door's sturdy support. "You are a piece of work, Liza Parrish. Not only do you not help the man, but you probably made him feel even worse."

Of course, after that encounter with Holden Kincaid, she wasn't feeling real whippy, either.

For several seconds, she stood there, her palms and forehead pressed against the wood. But then she caught a glimpse of movement through her front window and breathed out a resigned sigh when she saw Holden jogging down the sidewalk and disappearing into the night.

A warm, furry body brushed up against her legs, eliciting a smile and reminding Liza she wasn't completely alone. When she didn't immediately respond, Cruiser butted her nose beneath Liza's hand.

"What is it, girl?" Liza scratched the dog's ears as she pulled away from the door. The aging greyhound sat in Liza's path, twisting back one ear and staring up with her soft brown eyes. "No, I am not going to invite him inside for comfort food. And he's not that hot. We're like Romeo and Juliet—I'm not allowed to like him."

Cruiser turned and heeled beside her as Liza went into the kitchen to freshen their water for the night. Liza could almost imagine the dog communicating with her.

"Okay, so maybe he *is* hot, if you go for that square-jawed, clever, buttinsky type." Liza set the last dish on the floor and realized Bruiser had joined them—probably to see if there was anything new to eat in his dish. But Liza imagined he was giving her the same knowing look. "So he needs me to rescue him. I can't."

The greyhound cocked her head to one side while the terrier trotted forward, both responding to Liza's voice. "Don't look at me like that. Dogs, I can help. But Kincaid? His family?" She tapped the side of her head. "I'm kind of useless to them right now."

Great. Now Yukon appeared at the kitchen archway, checking to see what the discussion was all about. "Not you, too."

He walked his legs out in front of him and lay down. Like the others, his eyes and ears were attuned to every word. "We do not need a man in our lives—especially that one. I'll do what I can, but you have to forget that you ever met him." Liza frowned down at her three canine consciences. "I have to forget him, too."

MR. SMITH HUNG BACK IN the doorway, one hand tucked casually into the slacks pocket of his Prada suit. He was content to observe and evaluate until summoned. The older woman who'd called him away from his extended stay in the Cayman Islands strutted across the office toward the boss. He'd done work for both of them in the past, and had been paid handsomely for his expertise. He had no loyalty one way or the other, but he intended to end up on the winning side should this reunion not go well.

This was the first time in a long while that both of the big players in Z Group were together in the same room. Mr. Smith waited for the nostalgia to kick in. Once, their team had worked to maintain the status quo between hemispheres during the Cold War. Later, Z Group had infiltrated Communist Europe and helped pave the way for democracy. Those had been important times. It hadn't been all about the money back then.

Now, a generation of patriots had become movers and shakers in the world. Profiteers. The government had officially closed Z Group's covert operations when the Cold War had ended. But these two had seen an opportunity. With operatives in place, a market for arms and technology at the ready and secrecy assured, it had been a cakewalk to turn their talents into cash.

Would this East meets West meeting be a joining of forces? Or a clash of titans?

They greeted each other with smiles and traded hugs.

Nothing. But then, Mr. Smith didn't do misty-eyed and sentimental.

He'd stand back and watch these two take their trip

down memory lane, and silently place a bet as to which one of them really had the power these days, and would garner his loyalty.

"How did you get in?"

The older woman, looking as if she were poured into her expensive suit, laughed. "Your assistant believes I'm interviewing for the public relations position you advertised."

"I can't believe you're here." The boss gestured to a seat across the desk. "Are you sure it's safe to be in the United States again? What if someone recognizes you?"

"It's been thirty years since any of my old friends have seen me. Not even my own family would recognize me. No one knows who I am."

"John Kincaid did."

She smiled. It was as beautiful and cold as Mr. Smith remembered. "Yes, but who is he going to tell?"

Refusing to be baited, the boss unhooked the top button of his Armani jacket and sat. That one was a cool customer, too. As far as Mr. Smith could tell, this pissing match was dead even.

Instead of taking her seat, the woman leisurely circled the posh office, casually stroking her fingers behind the boss's crisp collar, then moving on to inspect photos and awards. "This is nice. I see you've done very well for yourself."

"I've earned it."

Mr. Smith pulled back his sleeve and checked the time. His gold Rolex stood out in sharp contrast against his dark skin. He wasn't worried about the time, or even nervous about the silence. Inspecting his nice things was just something he liked to do.

"Weren't my communiqués clear?" The boss sitting at

the desk broke the quiet first, indicating a defensiveness that tipped the balance of power to the curvy woman's favor. "I told you I've taken care of anyone who could possibly find out that Z Group still exists. James McBride, Laura Zook, Charlie Rogers, Leroy Maynard—"

"That's a lot of dead bodies in a short period of time."

"No one can trace the deaths back to me. I handled it like you did things in the old days. I recruited the talent I needed from prison to carry out each mission, and then eliminated them." The boss's blue-eyed gaze crossed the room to where Mr. Smith stood. "Or, I used people I can completely trust."

The woman's red lips curved with a sardonic laugh. "And who might that be, darling?"

Hands curled into fists, the boss rose behind the desk. "I've fooled the FBI and the local constabulary for months now. They have no idea that I'm connected to any of those crimes—or that you even exist."

"Overconfidence makes you foolish." Now the claws were coming out. "When John Kincaid's own son comes to Europe and starts digging up graves and running DNA tests, then that makes me think you're not getting the job done here."

"I gave *your* son, Tony Fierro, the job of finding out exactly what Atticus Kincaid and that mousy woman he now thinks he wants to marry knew about us. Tony screwed up and became the problem himself. I had to silence him as well."

If he was given to laughter, Mr. Smith would have guffawed at the irony. *He'd* been given the task of silencing Fierro. But apparently, Mommie Dearest felt no grief.

"Is there any wonder why I never claimed Tony as my own? He was eager to please, yes, but incompetent.

It shows *your* incompetence to rely on him." She waved her red-tipped nails toward the door. "That's why I called in Mr. Smith."

That was his cue to come all the way into the room. He pulled the manila envelope from beneath his arm and strode to the desk, looking down at both the woman he currently answered to, and the boss who'd paid for his services just a few short months ago.

"For what purpose? You can't kill Atticus Kincaid or any of his brothers. You'll have the whole of KCPD breathing down our necks, scrutinizing their every contact, every old girlfriend, every high-school buddy. I've had a profitable arrangement with the police department for several years now. I don't want to jeopardize that."

"Don't be so dramatic." The older woman finally sat, crossing her long legs and nodding to Mr. Smith to continue. "There's a simpler solution. Mr. Smith has already uncovered some information that you were unable to. Report."

Mr. Smith set the dossier of ten names on the desk top and pushed it across to the boss. "I've located the last of the Friedman Animal Clinic employees. Their addresses and phone numbers are there, as well as photographs so I can identify them on sight."

Sitting to peruse the file, the boss thumbed through the pages. "And we're certain the Friedman clinic is the one that was called to pick up that stray mutt the night we took care of John Kincaid?"

Mr. Smith nodded. His deep, theatrically-trained voice resonated through the office. "They're a private practice, not a public service unit. Unless there's a criminal action involved, beyond the initial phone call record and the health evaluation on the dog, they don't keep detailed reports after six months. So it's not clear who responded to the call. Only that one of their employees *was* in the dock area that night."

"My contacts at KCPD mentioned a possible witness. But if anyone came forward, their information must not have been enough to make an arrest." The boss closed the file and leaned back. "All three of us were there at that warehouse that night. It's been six months and the three of us are still here, still free. I haven't even been questioned. The witness must be unreliable, of no consequence."

The older woman laughed, but there was no humor. "Do you really want to risk that? According to your reports, Sawyer Kincaid was the first to discover there was a larger conspiracy involved in his father's murder—that it wasn't just a crime against a cop. Allowing that was your first mistake."

"I wanted to kill John outright," the boss argued. "You're the one who made it personal."

Ignoring the accusation, the older woman continued. "The information his brother, Atticus, uncovered could expose our entire operation—*if* he had a name or face to link it to."

The boss was no fool. "And this witness of yours might be able to provide that name or face, and give them a case." Mr. Smith felt the boss's scrutiny, felt the understanding that *he* was the final option who would make this entire mess go away. "And how, exactly, do you intend to narrow down the list of clinic employees and find out which one of them saw us that night?"

"Process of elimination. I intend to spice things up a bit. We'll see who the police work the hardest to protect. And that," concluded the woman, "will be our witness."

Mr. Smith nodded. "Within twenty-four hours of identification, that witness will be dead."

"No trace?" asked the boss.

The question was insulting. "I never leave a trace."

The boss grinned from ear to ear as though a giant weight had been lifted. "I like *dead.*"

Chapter Four

"Can you hear my voice, Liza?"

"Yes." Her voice was a drowsy murmur. The pillow behind her head was soft, the strains of New Age music filtering through her ears even softer.

"Tell me, what do you see?"

Blackness. Liza's hands fisted in the pillow she clutched over her stomach as a slight panic speared her.

"Shh. Easy, Liza. Don't be frightened. I'm right here with you." The scents of lavender and vanilla teased her nose. Some drowsy part of her mind suspected that Dr. Jameson had lit another one of those mood candles that, like the soft music and silk mask blocking the light, were meant to relax her. "Do you remember the eye mask you're wearing?" She nodded. "That's the blackness you see. Let it go and look further inside."

Liza pictured the black mask she wore and then shut it away in an imaginary box, the same way her therapist had instructed her to dismiss the other sensory objects in the room. As her initial panic subsided, she drifted back to that floaty place in her mind where sight and sound, taste and touch had no meaning.

"Now you're relaxed." Just when she thought she might actually fall asleep, the scent in the room changed, stinging her nose. The sweet smells became something dank and moldy, and suddenly she was back at the docks along the Missouri River, on one dark, fateful night when her life had changed.

Liza tensed, hearing the lap of the current against the dock pylons and rocky banks. She was moving through shadows, feeling the damp, uneven pavement of the run-down area beneath her running shoes as she searched each alley with her flashlight.

Directed dreaming, according to Dr. Jameson's research. He was stimulating her senses while in a suggestive state, guiding her mind toward a specific memory.

"Are you there, Liza?" Jameson asked quietly. "Do you see the warehouse?"

She nodded. "I hear him. Just a soft whimper. He doesn't come when I whistle. He doesn't bark." There. Two small orbs reflecting her light from beneath a Dumpster. "I see him. He's skin and bones. He's not getting up. He must be so afraid. Here, boy." She made a kissing sound twice with her lips. "Come here."

"Never mind the dog. The dog is fine. He's safe with you now." Yes. Bruiser recovered. He was fit and sassy and ruling the roost at her house. The doctor paused to let her shuffle the information in her mind and settle back into that relaxed, suggestive state. "After you found the dog that night, what happened?"

"I heard the explosion. Two explosions. Bruiser was so starved and dehydrated that he didn't even jump at the sound."

"Forget the damn dog." The slight edge in Dr. Jameson's voice crept into her consciousness. "Those were gunshots, Liza. What did you do when you heard the gunshots?"

"I hid." She flattened her back against the rough brick wall, crouching down behind a pile of stinky garbage bags. "I'm hugging the dog close and muzzling him with my hand so he doesn't make any noise. The pavement is wet."

"Are you afraid?"

"Yes."

"Why are you afraid?"

"I don't want them to see me."

"Who are you hiding from?"

"The men in the car." Where had the car come from? When did the men drive up? Her head was working in funny ways, skipping over chunks of time. Or maybe these were the only fragments she could remember.

"Can you see the car?"

"It's black. Big."

"I want you to move closer, Liza. Slide along the wall and get a better look. Be very quiet."

Obeying the command, she peeked through the narrow gaps between the plastic garbage bags.

"Do you see the car more clearly now?"

"Yes."

"What kind of car is it?"

"Big."

"Look closer. Do you see a logo? A word that tells you what kind of car it is?"

She squinted and leaned in. "There's a logo on the front grill. A circle with three flags or shields… Wait. It's a black Buick."

A shiver shook Liza on the couch as a black SUV very like the one that had nearly squished her on the road last night took shape in her mind. So powerful. So fast. So deadly.

"You're all right, Liza. No one can see you." Jameson wanted her to relax. "What does the license plate read?"

With the mix of memories, doors were slamming shut in her mind. "I can't see it."

"Take a deep breath and look again."

She shoved against one of the doors that was trying to close. "It's white. No, blue. It's white with a blue design on it."

"What do the letters say? The numbers? Look carefully."

Her knees felt scraped and wet as she scooted closer to the garbage. She lowered her gaze to the license plate. But a blinding pain flashed behind her eyes, as though she were looking straight into a pair of headlights. "I can't. I can't."

"Breathe deeply. In through your nose, out through your mouth." By the time she pulled back from the lights, that door in her memory had locked shut. But the questions were still coming. "Is anyone inside the car?"

"Two men."

"A white man and a black man?"

She'd been to this place before. Seen these men. Told this story. Why did she have to go back? "Yes."

"Is anyone else in the car with them?"

"Someone's getting in."

"Who?"

There was another flash of pain, another roadblock. "I don't know."

"What does he look like?"

"I can't see."

"Move closer. Take your time. Look harder."

"No. They'll hurt me if they see me. They'll hurt the dog if they find us." Fear, not clarity, snuck into her memories. Her head throbbed as she grew more agitated. The shadowy docks became an empty, blood-stained living room. She flashed back to the speeding SUV and diving for the curb. "The dog will try to protect me. They'll shoot him. I have to hide."

"They can't see you. Or the dog. Tell me about the man getting into the car."

"No." She was fidgeting, afraid, trapped in a blend of nightmares. Someone climbing into the back of the vehicle at the docks. A police officer in her parents' home, asking her to identify her slain parents and dog. Speeding cars. Seeing ghosts. Holden Kincaid on her front step, looking so like his father, demanding her help. "No!"

"*Liza.*" Her mother's voice. Gentle. Calming. Something to cling to when she was afraid.

"Mom?"

Liza felt a jarring touch on her hand and snatched it away. "Your mother's not there, Liza. Stay with me. Stay in the alley. Tell me what you see."

"*Stay away, sweetie. It isn't safe.*"

"Mom? I have to help. I want to help."

"Damn it. I've lost her." Trent Jameson wasn't talking to her anymore. He used a sharper, clipped tone to speak into his tape recorder. "Subject is reverting back to earlier memory. May look into drug trials to keep her in relaxed, focused state."

"Dr. Jameson?" She called to him, reaching for a steadying hand to guide her through the chaos in her head.

"Relax." The sonorous monotone had returned. "Go back to the quiet place. Tell me who is getting in the car, Liza."

But in her mind, the car was gone. The foggy windows and faceless figures inside had gone with it.

New images were battering her now. She was inside the warehouse, kneeling beside the dead body, watching the pool of blood expand beneath the man's head. "He's dead."

"Go back to the car, Liza."

"Stay back, sweetie. It isn't safe."

"I need you. Good night, Parrish." Holden Kincaid's strong arms and soothing voice dissipated almost as soon as they appeared.

Then she was reaching down to feel John Kincaid's pulse. His skin was cold and clammy and still. Tears burned in her eyes at the cruelty of his death. His face was so familiar. But the square jaw was discolored. Broken. "I want to help you," she cried. "I'm trying."

"Liza. I need you to go back to the men in the car."

"Stay away. It isn't safe."

"I'm sorry I couldn't help you, Mom. I'm sorry I wasn't there to keep you and Dad safe."

"Liza—"

"It isn't safe."

"I need you."

"I have to help. I have to remember."

"Yes. Remember. Tell me about—"

The dead man grabbed her hand. *"Remember!"*

Liza screamed herself fully awake. She tore off her mask and sat up, wincing as even the dim light from candles and behind drawn shades seared her sensitive eyes. Her head ached, and she felt disoriented.

Feeling like an abject failure because her mind refused to cooperate, she picked up the pillow that had rolled to the floor and set it back on the couch in an apologetic need to straighten out the literal and figurative mess she had made. "I'm sorry."

Dr. Jameson didn't look up from his notes for several moments. When he did, his rueful smile made him appear gravely disappointed—or maybe that was pity. "Headache?"

Liza massaged her temples, feeling sick to her stomach, from the intense pain. "Nasty one."

"I told you to let me wake you up slowly. The jump from a hypnotic state to waking consciousness is too abrupt."

That was more fatherly rebuke than sympathetic support. "But it's so frightening. So frustrating." Liza stopped the massage that wasn't helping anyway. "Did I remember anything new?"

"You confirmed the make of the car you saw that night. A Buick. But then you skipped to discovering the body. And you revisited your parents' murders again."

"I heard my mother's voice. She told me to 'stay away.' From the gruesome sight of John Kincaid's body, I guess." Not that the warning had worked. Why couldn't she forget *that* most heartbreaking part of the crime she'd witnessed?

Even though she'd like to talk a little more, her session time was apparently over. Dr. Jameson was checking the calendar on his phone. "I'm more convinced than ever that the memories are there. That you did see something significant that night, but that you're blocking it. When I asked about the license plate, you mentioned a door closing."

"The car door?"

"The door blocking that memory. And the memory of what the men inside the car looked like. I believe we're on the brink of discovery—of breaking this wide open." She wished his optimism was contagious. "I want to review the transcript from this session, organize my thoughts, then try this again tomorrow."

"Tomorrow?"

He punched in numbers with his stylus. "Are you free?"

She had school, had a job, had a life. But mostly, she needed time to regroup from this raw, vulnerable feeling. "I was hoping to have a few days off to relax. This is scary for me. I mean, I want to know, but then, I'm afraid to know."

"I can cancel my lunch appointment if that's the only time you're free."

This was the place for therapy, not sympathy, apparently. "I can't take a break?"

"I don't want you to regress any. We are right on the edge of a breakthrough. I can feel it."

She wished she could. "I really think I need the time to—"

"I know your nightmares torment you, Liza. And you believe that if you could just remember everything the police want you to that you could put it out of your mind." It was a cruel reminder, but the doctor softened it by pulling her to her feet and wrapping an arm around her shoulders as he walked her toward his office door. "It's the searching for answers, for closure, that keeps the nightmares coming back. You know I'm your best chance at unlocking those hidden places inside your head. The longer you delay, the longer the nightmares will continue. Do you want that?"

"Of course not." Feeling uncharacteristically drained of fight, Liza grabbed her backpack. "Between my morning seminar and work at the clinic tomorrow afternoon, I'll stop by."

"I'll see you at noon?"

"Sure." He opened the door for her and she headed out, feeling a little jittery—like she'd been up studying all night for exams and was subsisting on caffeine rather than sleep. "Dr. Jameson? Be honest. Am I getting any better? Do you think I'll ever remember everything?"

"Hypnosis isn't an exact science, dear. But we're making such good progress, I'm hopeful that yes, we'll eventually unlock all of those memories inside your head." He stopped at the outer door and finally gave her the reassurance of an indulgent smile. "At the very least, I promise that I'll make the nightmares go away."

Liza appreciated the sentiment. But as she walked to the elevators at the end of the hall, she could only think of one thing. She didn't have to be asleep to be haunted by nightmares. And until she could remember who'd killed John Kincaid, she doubted Dr. Jameson's claim was a promise he could keep.

"WHAT DO YOU MEAN, WEIRD things are happening?" Liza held the bull terrier still on top of the clinic's metal examination table while her friend, vet tech Anita Logan, swabbed a medicated ointment over the dog's skin rash.

"That's it, Marvin. Good boy." Anita praised the dog for his calm behavior. Already a good-natured animal, he seemed grateful for the soothing relief that a bath, tests and medicine had given him. As Anita stooped down to tend to a patch on the dog's belly, she continued. "I'm just sayin'. Lots of unusual things have been happenin' to the people who work here. My granny would say we're under a bad star."

Liza frowned. "Define 'lots.'"

"All done." Anita pulled a pen from her lab coat pocket

and jotted the name and application time on the dog's chart. "Well, there was you and that crazy SUV driver you told me about. Dr. Friedman said someone egged her car last night. Then, this morning, Reynaldo came in and said somebody had vandalized his mailbox last night— shot it all up. He and his family were all at Wednesday church services, so no one was hurt. But still…"

"That's a relief no one was injured." Liza set Marvin on the floor, looped a lead around his neck and headed for the kennel area in the back room.

"And this morning…" Anita pitched her trash and followed, waiting until they were alone in the back to finish. "This morning, I could swear this guy was following me."

Liza opened one of the lower cages and put Marvin inside before removing the lead and closing the cage door. "Didn't you take the bus?"

"You know I did. I can't afford parking *and* gas these days." Anita was playing with the black lab mix in the cage next to Marvin's. The flawless caramel skin at her forehead was creased with a frown. "That's just it. I saw this man on the bus—somebody new, not from the neighborhood. I caught him staring at me more than once."

"Maybe he was hitting on you."

"If he was, he's not my type. He was a *big* brother. Shaved head, goatee."

The man sitting behind the wheel of that SUV last night had been big. But no, what kind of connection could there be between Anita's story and Scary Man with the headlights? Liza managed to keep the frisson of foreboding that crawled through her veins out of her voice. "That doesn't sound too bad. Did he say something crude? Was he wearing a wedding ring?"

Anita pulled her fingers away from the dog and shook her head. "I didn't want to look that close. He just stared. Never said a word, never smiled. It creeped me out. Especially when he got off at the same stop."

"He followed you to the clinic? He didn't try to accost you, did he?"

"No. He came right up behind me, like he wanted to try something, but he walked on past. And Liza, girl—this is the really weird part—when I went to Snow's Barbecue for lunch, I swear I saw him standing across the street, watching me again."

"You're sure it was the same man?"

Anita's dramatic shiver rippled from head to toe. "Girl, you don't forget that kind of scary. It was him."

Liza's life had grown disturbing enough over the past six months without hearing that her friends were being victimized as well. She reached out to rub a supportive hand up and down Anita's arm. "Do you think you need to call the police?"

Anita snorted. "And tell them what?"

Detective Grove had asked plenty of questions about what she'd seen at that warehouse, so Liza knew the routine. "Give them a description. Tell them where he got on the bus and where he got off. That you saw him again at the restaurant. Tell them he scared you."

"They don't arrest a man for lookin' tough."

"No, but if his description fits some other crime—or if they can link him to the same kind of report from other women—KCPD would want to know that."

Holden Kincaid, Kevin Grove and the rest of KCPD would love to have such a detailed description about a possible suspect. They'd be more pleased with the accuracy of Anita's description and would probably have more patience with her than they did with Liza's vague report.

A little bit of the headache that had throbbed for an hour after leaving her lunchtime session with Dr. Jameson began to rap at her temples.

"You all right, girl?" Anita's concern startled Liza, and she wondered how long she'd stood there, trapped inside her own thoughts.

Liza combed her fingers through her hair, mussing up the copper fringe and buying herself a moment to summon a reassuring smile. "I've just got a bit of a headache, I guess. Probably another manifestation of your granny's 'bad star.'"

"Maybe." Anita accepted the excuse, even if her light brown eyes showed that she didn't believe it. She opened the door to the main room and pointed toward the reception area. "Linda keeps some ibuprofen in her desk. Why don't you take a couple and find an empty room to lie down in for a few minutes. I know you're burning the candle at both ends."

Liza eyed the stack of treatment charts on the counter that Dr. Friedman had asked her to review. "I've got work to do."

Anita took her by the shoulders and nudged her toward the front desk. "Granny may be superstitious, but I'm not. I'm tired of all this craziness, but a headache I can deal with. Now go take care of yourself. We can manage without you for ten minutes back here."

"Are you sure?"

"Go."

Smiling her thanks, Liza wove her way through the examination tables and lab counters to the front room. Liza spotted their receptionist, Linda, through the front windows, huddled in her jacket and smoking a cigarette with one of their community volunteers. Trading a wave to let the receptionist know she'd was borrowing her desk for a few minutes, Liza sat behind the counter and opened the desk's main drawer. "Let's see. Ibuprofen, ibuprofen…"

As she rummaged her way through the drawer, the telephone rang. Linda was still in the middle of an animated conversation outside, so before the phone ended its second ring, Liza picked it up and answered. "Friedman Animal Clinic."

"Get out of the building."

The voice was so low that Liza questioned whether she had heard right. "Excuse me?"

"Get out of the building."

An icy finger touched the nape of her neck and pricked goose bumps across her skin beneath her sweater and lab coat. "Who is this?"

"Get out."

"Why?"

"There's a bomb."

HOLDEN LIFTED HIS FATHER'S ten-speed bicycle off the ceiling hooks in the garage and handed it down the ladder to Bill Caldwell. "Got it?"

"I've got it."

The tires were flat and the rubber around the rims sticky from years of disuse. Still, they handled the old bike as reverently as a newborn baby—because it had been John's.

"Where do you want it, Su?" Bill asked, squeezing between Holden's mother and a stack of boxes she'd packed with some of her late husband's clothes. "With the boxes you're donating to the church for their Christmas bazaar? Or in the back of my truck to go to the city mission?"

Susan tucked a sable-colored strand of hair back into her ponytail and pointed to the corner of the garage. "There'll be some child who wants a bike for Christmas, and after the men's group fixes it up, it'll make a perfect gift."

Holden looked down from his perch and watched Bill dip his head to kiss Susan. "Spoken like a true mother. John would be pleased to see a little boy putting this bike to good use again."

"I think so, too."

Interesting. Was his mother blushing? Bill Caldwell seemed to be stealing several pecks on the cheek or lips lately. More than he'd done when Holden's father was still alive. It wasn't uncommon for Caldwell to greet Susan with a kiss. After all, John Kincaid had often given a friendly hug or kiss to Bill's late wife, Erin, when they met. But now there was something subtly different about their interaction that made Holden want to trade places with Bill and put a little hands-off distance between the two sixty-year-olds.

Not that he begrudged his parents' generation the right to be attracted to someone. His mother and Bill had a lot in common beyond their ties to Holden's father. Susan Kincaid was a smart, loving, beautiful woman, and Bill Caldwell—with those distinguished silver sideburns and a multinational technology business that he'd built from the ground up—was probably a pretty good catch himself. If their friendship evolved into something more, Holden couldn't stop it.

He just didn't have to like how quickly the new relationship seemed to be progressing. How could they move on to something new when his father's murder hadn't even been solved yet?

He shook off the uncharitable feelings and turned to straighten a box of books. "What are you, eight or twenty-eight?" he chided himself. Bill and his mother had both lost their very best friend. Who was he to fault them for being drawn together now that they were both alone?

He hoped when *he* was older he would have the right woman by his side to keep things interesting.

Hmm. Did copper-red hair turn gray, silver or white when it aged?

"Oh hell." Holden nearly tipped the ladder as that random thought caught him by surprise. He thought he'd put Liza Parrish firmly out of his mind. Maybe he'd better climb down before he hurt himself.

While Holden descended and put away the ladder, he discovered that his thoughts would go where they wanted to go. Back to Liza.

This afternoon's irritability probably had something to do with the sweet, round bottom that had tumbled into his lap last night. Dogs and bruises aside, he'd been very much aware of curves and warmth, and the way the moonlight reflected in her silvery eyes and made them sparkle. Her lips were a natural shade of peach, adorned with nothing but lip balm. They moved with a fascinating agility when she argued, which was often. And despite his nobler instincts, he'd wondered if her lips would be equally agile if silenced with a kiss.

Beyond the unexpected sexual attraction he felt toward KCPD's prime witness, he'd been thrown even further off his game twenty minutes later when he'd gotten a glimpse of the frightened, vulnerable woman lurking beneath that tough-chick facade. Liza Parrish had no problem standing up and fighting for herself, but once the adrenaline of fear and bravado had worn off, she'd collapsed into his arms and clung to his hand like a woman who needed him. That unspoken request had tapped into something far deeper inside him than the simmering mix of frustration and desire that had kept him awake late into the morning hours.

He'd finally been able to fall asleep. But then he'd been plagued by a variety of erotic dreams that involved rolling around on the ground, heated kisses and finding out whether those freckles that dusted her cheeks covered the rest of her body as well.

Yeah, right. He had no business judging his mother's taste in a new partner, when he seemed to have made an unplanned and ill-advised choice himself. Liza Parrish was forbidden fruit. He couldn't afford to be tempted. Finding the truth about his father's murder—finding peace—might depend on his ability to keep his distance from her.

"Do you need me to move anything else for you, Mom?" Susan Kincaid had invited him to stop by when she was done teaching her high-school English classes. Beyond the opportunity to check on her, which he and his brothers did frequently, Holden had willingly agreed to trade a little muscle for one of her home-cooked meals. "If not, maybe I can get some of those leaves raked up in the yard before dinner."

"Are you sure?" She came over to pat him on the stomach, then stretched up on tiptoe to kiss his jaw. "My intention was to fatten you up a bit on my pot roast and spend some quality time with you, not work you like a slave-driver."

"I don't mind, Mom." Holden grinned and dipped his head to kiss his mother's cheek. "I'm more than happy to work for your pot roast."

He heard the crunch of tires on the driveway and spotted a familiar, if rarely seen, beat-up green Jeep Cherokee pull in, even before Bill Caldwell announced its arrival. "I'll be damned." He closed the back of his truck and went to greet Holden's oldest brother, Edward. "Look what the cat dragged in. How're you doin', son?"

Edward climbed out of the Jeep, his worn jeans and black sweater a familiar uniform of late. Edward considered questions like "How are you?" or "How do you feel?" to be rhetorical, and never answered them. But he did shake Bill's hand. "It's been a long time, Bill."

"Edward." Susan hurried ahead of Holden, her arms outstretched as she pushed past Bill and wrapped Edward up in a tight maternal hug. "Oh, sweetie, it's so good to see you."

He bent his head and hugged her back, hanging on just long enough for Holden to join the group. He extended a hand behind her back and straightened. "Little brother. Mooching a free meal?"

Holden grasped his hand, relieved to feel the strength in his brother's grip. "I'm earning my keep."

Susan pulled away, studying her reclusive son from head to toe. "Let me look at you."

Holden took the same opportunity to assess Edward's ongoing recovery from the tragedy that had not only wrecked his body, but had destroyed his soul. Edward hadn't shaved for a day or so, and the dark stubble made a smattering of scars along his jawline stick out like brands. Though a smile would be hard to come by, there were no circles beneath his eyes and his color was a healthy tan, indicating he was continuing to stay sober. He didn't reach inside the Jeep for his thick, walnut cane until he was ready to close the door. Was it Holden's imagination, or was Edward's limp even less pronounced than when he'd last seen him three weeks ago?

Outwardly, at least, John Kincaid's firstborn was on the mend.

"You look good, son." Susan's gentle smile had healing powers that even Edward wasn't immune to. "I wasn't sure you'd come, but I'm so glad you're here."

Edward leaned in to accept her kiss. "I smelled your pot roast a mile away, Mom."

Susan reached for Holden's hand and pulled him forward. "Holden, will you help your brother unload his truck? He's got some things he wants to move out of his house. I said I'd put them in with my church donations."

"Sure." He gestured to the back of the Jeep. "Lead on, Macduff."

While her oldest and youngest sons moved to the rear of Edward's vehicle, Susan linked her arm through Bill Caldwell's and led him back inside the garage. "You come with me to the kitchen and toss together a salad while I get the roast and veggies out of the slow cooker. I have to set another place for dinner."

After Edward opened the back hatch, Holden reached inside for a pile of clothes, still on their hangers in plastic bags from the dry cleaners. Holden hesitated for a second before scooping up the first armful. These were Cara's things. Edward's late wife had been petite and curvy, a dynamo of a woman who'd left a successful career in business to become a full-time mother. Her colorful, classy tastes were reflected in the stylish suits and dresses.

It must have been hell for Edward to finally empty his wife's closet. Holden picked up the entire stack and carried them for his brother. No need to ask why Edward wanted to get rid of them.

He carried in a box of jeans and casual clothes, and a little girl's bike that had never been ridden.

Holden tried to distract his brother from the painful parade of memories. He talked about Chiefs football, and Atticus's trip to Sarajevo with Brooke. He mentioned how it felt to be working under Mitch Taylor, the new precinct commander who now oversaw the Fourth, and how he often asked about Edward and when he planned to return to his work as an investigator. He even asked a curious question of his own. "So, what do you think about Mom and Bill getting to be such good friends?"

"We'll see."

Conversation with Edward was a minimalist thing, so Holden didn't push for answers.

Until he saw in the backseat the open box he was supposed to carry in next. A shaggy blond head with sweet blue eyes blipped into Holden's memory and twisted his heart. He'd often volunteered to assist Edward in coaching his niece's track and kickball teams.

He stopped Edward on his way to the garage. "These are Melinda's things. Her Special Olympics participation medals, some artwork from school. Christmas decorations. You're not getting rid of these, are you?"

"I don't need you to be my conscience, little brother."

"I'm talking common sense. Even Mom isn't getting rid of all of Dad's things." Holden knew he was treading on mighty thin ice here. But somebody needed to say this. "You can't just erase your wife and child from your life, Ed. What if you get to the time when you've moved on, and you could treasure some of these sentimental items but you've given them away to strangers? Wouldn't you feel the loss all over again?"

"Move on?" Edward turned away from the box and leaned on his cane with both hands, seeming to need its support now more than he had a minute ago. "Every damn day it's a chore to get up in the morning. And when I do I figure that means I'm moving on the way that grief counselor told me to. I try to stay busy. I've fixed up the house. I fixed the damn Jeep. And I think I'm doing okay, that I'm gonna make it." Edward turned, and Holden saw a look of such bleak pain in his brother's eyes, that he backed up half a step. Edward limped forward. "But then I go up into the attic to get a storm window, or I open a storage closet in the basement and I run across something of Cara's or Melinda's, and I'm back on that Christmas Eve morning. It's a matter of survival, Holden." His cane punctuated his sentence on the concrete beside Holden's foot. "They have to go."

Well, hell. Holden could get all tough and in-your-face, too. But it was harder just to listen, and to love. He reached into the box and pulled out a hand-sewn rag doll ornament with plastic eyes glued crookedly on its face. An odd present to give a man like Edward Kincaid, but because his daughter had made it herself, Edward had loved it. "You're not giving *this* to some stranger."

Edward swiped his hand across his jaw, taking all trace of emotion with it. He tapped his cane against the box. "It all goes."

Because he wasn't about to lie to his brother, Holden simply nodded. He set the doll ornament back into the box, then carried it into the garage—setting it well away from the boxes that were going to the church. He'd tell his mom later. *She'd* want to keep the sentimental things. If Edward did want them one day, she'd be more than happy to give them back.

After a few minutes of silence Edward's mood seemed to come back into the tolerable range, and Holden offered a suggestion. "You know, if you're looking for something to do to stay busy, come work out with me at the gym. I've found that physical exertion has been a pretty fair antidote to deal with losing Dad. And staying healthy's always a good thing."

With his Jeep now empty, Edward locked it up. "I'll think about it."

Holden slowed his pace to walk side by side into the garage. "You could always go back to work. Maybe get your private investigator's license if the badge doesn't suit you anymore. You could help Sawyer and Atticus and me find the man who killed Dad and broke Mom's heart. If the four of us worked together as a team, we could get that bastard."

"I thought that investigation was off-limits to Kincaids. I know Sawyer uncovered some circumstantial evidence that the lab has, and Atticus has been nosing around in Dad's journals, looking at his work with Z Group before Dad became a cop. But they've turned all that over to the police." Those piercing gray eyes could still do a knowing big-brother look. "You're a sharpshooter, not an investigator. So what are you up to?"

Holden shoved his hands into the pockets of his jeans before he answered. "I, uh, went and had a chat with a witness who was there that night."

Edward's hand on his arm stopped him. "You're kidding, right?"

"I just wanted to know why she won't open up about what she saw, and give us some kind of break on the case."

"She?"

"Liza Parrish." He skipped the description of freckles and curves and keeping him up at night. "She's scared of something. Or someone. I saw a car nearly run her down last night. I don't know if it's connected. I ran the plates and it came up a rental car. Maybe if we could assign a bodyguard to make her feel safe, then she'd feel it was okay to open up and talk."

"You think she's in danger?" Despite the fact his gun and badge were packed up in a drawer somewhere, Edward still thought like a cop. "Did you notify the OIC of your suspicions?"

The OIC—Officer in Charge of the investigation—Kevin Grove, would have his hide if he knew Holden had already made personal contact—lots of contact—with the witness. "You think I should?"

"Hell, yes. If she can break open Dad's case, we want her in one piece." Edward frowned at Holden's uncharacteristic silence. "Is there something more going on here? Did something else happen between you and that woman?"

The phone on Holden's belt vibrated, saving him from having to answer.

He flipped open his phone, recognized Lieutenant Cutler's number. "Lieutenant? What's up?"

Mike Cutler's clipped tone confirmed that this was no social call. "We've got a situation in the 1100 block of South Broadway. Someone called in a bomb threat to the Friedman Animal Clinic."

When he'd done his research on Liza Parrish, he'd found out that she was working an internship at that same clinic. Cars gunning for her in the middle of the street? Bomb threats? He wouldn't buy any coincidence theory.

The instinct to get to Liza jolted through his limbs. But he wasn't supposed to know about her. He wasn't supposed to care whether or not she was safe. He grit his teeth and ignored the distracting impulses. "That's bomb squad's department."

"Not when we've got a perp in the building across the street firing shots into the crowd of evacuees, on-lookers and official vehicles."

Holden swore. "Any casualties?"

"Not yet. But we're up, big guy. Is your head back in the game yet? We need to do a sweep of the building across the street."

Holden put his hand over the phone and looked at Edward. "Will you stay with Mom? Tell her I'm gone?"

He nodded. "Go save the day, little brother."

Pulling his keys from his pocket and dashing toward his Mustang, Holden put the phone back to his ear. "I'm on my way."

Chapter Five

"Clear!"

After Dominic Molloy gave him the signal, Holden turned the corner around the last of the air-conditioning units. Leading with his Glock, he checked between the exhaust vents and outer wall. With no shooter in sight, he announced it was safe for Dom to proceed. "Clear!"

Holden watched his partner's back while Dom peered over the edge of the building. "Clear! The next building's roof is eight stories below us. If the shooter had jumped, I'd see a body."

It was probably safe to breathe easier now, but both men had been trained not to drop their guard until they were back at the van stowing their gear. Holden had one last wall to check. With the sunset at his back, he followed his own shadow to the front side of the building and looked over the edge to the street below. South Broadway was a four-lane street with bus lanes, parking and sidewalks on either side. No way would the shooter have risked a jump like that unless he thought he could fly. "Clear!"

He nodded to Dominic.

With an answering nod, Dom lowered his weapon

and tapped the microphone inside his helmet to broadcast to their entire unit. "Roof's clear, lieutenant. The perp must have gotten out with the last of the tenants when we evacuated."

"Understood. I'm waiting to hear from Trip and Delgado in the basement."

Holden lowered his Glock, noting how easy it would be to shatter the animal clinic's front window from this position. The shooter had, too. Hitting a target inside the ground-level clinic would be impossible from this height, but anything on the street would be fair game.

A man with a high-powered rifle would be untouchable this high up unless they had a chopper. Holden touched his black-gloved fingers to the ledge near a trio of powder burns where the shooter had rested his rifle. But he'd policed his brass like a pro. There were no casings on the roof, not so much as a gum wrapper to give any indication of the terror that had rained down just a half hour earlier.

"This guy's good," Holden reported.

Dominic walked up beside him. "Yeah, well, if he's so damn good, why didn't he hit anybody? Not that I'm askin' for trouble, but there were civilians, cops, EMTs, reporters all on the street before we got the area completely closed off. How come all he hit was a window, a bus and a couple of traffic lights?"

Holden crouched down and put himself in the shooter's position. Even now, as uniformed officers kept bystanders and reporters more than a block away, he could adjust the angle of the weapon and make a difficult but doable shot and take out the driver of the television news van and two traffic cops.

"What are you thinkin', big guy?"

"That our shooter hit exactly what he aimed at."

Dominic chomped his gum and frowned. "So what's the point of calling in a fake bomb to get all these targets on the street, and then miss them on purpose?"

"That's what I'd like to know." Had he been gunning for someone in particular? Like a mouthy redhead with fear in her eyes? "Maybe he didn't spot his intended target so he fired wildly to throw us off track."

"Or maybe he just wanted to throw a scare into somebody."

Holden glanced down at his buddy. Dom's off-the-cuff intuition was usually amazingly accurate. And bad guys *did* like to scare witnesses who might testify against them. Holden was already backing toward the roof entrance. "Did we clear the clinic across the street?"

"Bomb squad did." Dom followed behind him. "Our shooter's long gone."

"Basement's clear." Lieutenant Cutler's voice sounded inside their helmets, ending Holden's intent to run across the street and find Liza. He still had work to do. "Report back to 517. I want to take this room apart before we turn it over to the lab guys."

"On our way."

The secondary location where the bomb threat call had been made from wasn't an apartment so much as a bunch of empty rooms—rented for the week and paid for in cash. There was a card table, a folding chair and a telephone, and not a damn clue as to the perp's identity.

Dominic snickered at the name scrawled inside the building manager's registry. "You honestly think our perp's name was Johann Hart?"

Holden was leaning against the window frame, watching as a team of crime scene investigators ducked beneath the yellow tape marking off the animal clinic.

Uniformed officers were also beginning to let some of the clinic workers back in, assuming that was who the four men and women in the white lab coats were.

Like the others on his S.W.A.T. team, he'd removed his helmet and holstered his gun, standing down from full alert. They now wore their ball caps and some pretty conflicted expressions over a dangerous suspect who'd escaped them.

Razzing from the others drew Holden's focus back into the room as Dominic waved a copy of the registration page in the air. "Hello? Johann, John. A hart's a deer, a doe's a deer. John Doe?"

Trip shook his head. "How long did it take you to think that one up?"

"This guy's a ghost," Delgado griped. "We'll never find him."

"Focus, people," Cutler ordered. "Our shooter's in the wind. Unless we dig up a gun in this apartment, I'm going to assume he smuggled the weapon out somehow, and that he's armed and dangerous."

A shock of copper-red caught Holden's attention as Liza ducked beneath the tape to hurry after the other clinic workers. Ah, hell. Not only was that hair as good as a neon sign to aim at, even through the lengthening twilight shadows, but he'd spotted a television reporter and her cameraman pleading with one of the officers to let her in to the crime scene.

Holden was going to jump out of his skin if he couldn't do something about the train wreck he saw coming. "May I be excused from the search, sir?"

Cutler's blue eyes narrowed, no doubt assessing the unusual request. "Is there a problem?"

"I need to take care of something."

The lieutenant deliberated for a few seconds, then dismissed him. "Go. If you see something, you get on the horn and call it in."

"Yes, sir."

HOLDEN SKIPPED THE ELEVATOR and took the stairs two at a time down to the street. He pushed open the front doors in time to see TV reporter Hayley Resnick and her cameraman being pushed back out of the clinic by a testy female CSI. When the reporter stuck her microphone in the CSI's face and asked her to comment on the situation, the tall brunette turned and followed Holden into the building.

"Just stay clear of the bullet holes in the front desk and counter," she warned, hurrying past him. "The back of the building is clear, but I've got my people pulling a couple of slugs here."

Deciding that a response was neither wanted nor necessary, Holden headed toward the back where he could hear several voices—including Liza's. His boots crunched over the glass on the floor, but as the CSI had indicated, it appeared that all the damage was relegated to the very front of the clinic.

"…not bringing the dogs back here tonight, are we?"

"No. We'll leave them in the Sterling and Wyandotte shelters for tonight. Anita, make sure we have the charts for the acute cases."

Holden followed the voices through a swinging door into a lab and examination area. An older woman was directing her staff. "I already have Liza securing the pharmacy. I'm not going to risk any break-ins tonight. Reynaldo, I need you to…"

With an acknowledging salute, Holden left them to

their work and pushed open the door marked "Pharmacy." He shouldn't have breathed a sigh of relief when he saw Liza's heart-shaped bottom wiggling in the air as she bent over an open cooler, but he did.

She popped up, startled by the sound. Her pale cheeks were flushed when she spun around. "Kincaid? You're not supposed to be here."

Though she held her defiant chin high, the tension on her face made her mouth stiff, her eyes a dull battleship gray.

Holden never paused, never broke stride. He walked straight across the room, pulled off his black S.W.A.T. cap and plopped it onto her head, tugging it securely over the short wisps of her hair.

"Red hair makes an easy target."

He wasn't the only one breathing a sigh of relief. A smile suited those pretty lips better than that tough survivor frown had. "Is it wrong to say I'm glad to see you?"

"I hope not. Because the feeling's mutual." His answering smile faded when he reached out to touch the nick on her cheek with the tip of his finger. "Are you hurt?"

He could have sworn her skin trembled beneath his touch, but she pulled away so quickly he couldn't be sure.

"We all have little cuts and bumps." She went back to pulling bottles of pills and liquids off the shelves and packing them into the cooler. "We were still evacuating the last of the big dogs onto the transport truck when that crazy man—I mean, I'm assuming it was a man—shot out the main window. But the EMTs checked us out. There were no serious injuries."

"Did you see the shooter?"

She paused for a moment, then made a sound that wasn't quite a laugh. "Not this time."

Her skin had gone pale beneath its dusting of freckles as she stretched up to get a second cooler off the top of the medicine cabinet. Holden moved in behind her, easily reaching over her head to retrieve the cooler. "Let me."

As she rocked back onto her heels, she butted up against Holden's chest. He heard a sharp catch of breath—maybe it was Liza's, maybe it was his own. He was instantly aware of a chest-to-groin heat that seared through his flak vest and clothes. He should have retreated. Instead, he propped the cooler against the wall with one hand and pulled her close to ease any lingering doubts he might have that she was unharmed.

But Liza had a saner notion of propriety and protocol. With an unnecessary apology, she ducked beneath his arm and scooted away to open a refrigerator door. Holden set the smaller cooler on top of the first one, and stepped aside to let her fill it with vials from the fridge.

"I *did* take the phone call when the bomb threat came in. That was definitely a man's voice. It was low-pitched and resonant, like yours, but…" she paused with her fist resting on the top shelf "…cold. Like there was no emotion there whatsoever."

She pulled the last of the meds out and nudged the door shut with her hip, suddenly energized, suddenly apologizing.

"Your voice isn't like that at all. It has a warmth to it. It can be annoying, but, that's usually *what* you're saying. When it's soft, the tone of it is almost… soothing." She was that close to being dead and she was worried about hurting *his* feelings? The lurch in Holden's stomach felt a lot more personal than the idea of losing a link to his father's murder.

"This guy sounded like Shakespeare-meets-the-Terminator, but you could be a—"

"It's all right, Parrish." He caught her jaw beneath his palm, stopping the rambling apology—and the deeper sense of fear and uncertainty she was revealing. He stroked his thumb across the point of her chin. "It's all right."

Her eyes sparkled with some unnamed emotion. "Is it? I've seen so much violence, I can't... How do you handle it?"

He needed her to be out of this place. Now. He needed Liza somewhere safe.

"Come on." The instant Liza closed the top cooler, he pushed it into her hands. Then he picked up the larger one. "Where do these go?"

"Dr. Friedman parked her van in the back. This way."

He followed her down a hallway lined with kennels to the back door. But he stopped her before she could open it.

"Wait." He stacked the coolers on the floor and reached for the Velcro straps at either side of his black flak vest.

"What are you doing?" He pulled the vest over his head and dropped it over hers in one smooth motion. "Kincaid?"

He straightened his cap on her head and reached around her to secure the straps over her white lab coat. "There's a guy with a gun out there, remember?"

She ripped open a strap in protest. "But it's okay for you to get shot?"

"I wasn't the target." He covered her hand and latched the strap.

Whether his words or his touch bothered her, he couldn't tell. But she quickly pulled away and picked up her cooler. "You think he was shooting at me? Putting all these innocent animals and people into danger because of me?"

"It's too soon to tell." She swam in his vest, like a little girl playing dress-up in her daddy's clothes. But to Holden's mind, it was a good fit. "Silencing or scaring a murder witness so that she won't testify? Wouldn't be the first time." Holden opened the door and headed into the alley. "Stay close."

She followed right on his heels, opening the back of the van and showing him where to store the medical supplies. "I heard at least six shots. That guy wasn't shooting at me. Other than the front window, he never came close. Unless he's a lousy shot."

"He wasn't."

"How do you know?"

He slammed the van shut and turned on her. "Because *I'm* a sharpshooter. I saw his setup. I saw the shots he could take and the ones he did take. He's trained. Military, cop, hit man, I don't know. If he wanted you dead right now, you would be. This is some game he's playing, and I'm not going to take the chance that *you're* the one he wants in the middle of it."

She propped her hands at her hips, squaring off against him. "Because I need to stay alive to testify against your father's killer?"

"Because you need to stay alive, period."

"Look, we hardly know each other. What right—?"

It was a bright light, not a gunshot that stopped the debate. "Doctor?"

Liza squinted and turned toward the television camera. "Me? Not quite yet. But Dr. Friedman's inside if you need a vet."

Holden took Liza's arm and pulled her behind him,

putting his body between her and the blond reporter. "Get that camera out of here."

"I'm Hayley Resnick, Channel 4 News. Could I ask you some questions?" With a strength of will that belied her movie-star pretty face, she darted to one side and focused her plea on Liza. "Miss? Were you a victim of the bomb threat? Can you tell us anything about why someone would target these defenseless animals or someone who works here?"

Holden felt Liza's response in the clench of her fists at the back of his shirt. "You think this is about the animals?" she whispered.

"No, I don't. Hey!" Holden adjusted his stance, pushing Hayley back and giving her cameraman the high sign to kill the light and stop rolling the film. "This isn't a good time for an interview."

But Hayley kept pushing. "So this is personal? Have you received threats before?"

"I'm supposed to remain anonymous," Liza spoke against his shoulder. "Detective Grove promised."

Holden stretched his arms behind him, hugging Liza to his back and turning to keep her hidden. "There are others who can give you better information about today's events, Ms. Resnick. I suggest you try elsewhere."

The reporter shifted her attention to Holden, gracing him with a practiced smile. "You're Atticus's brother, aren't you?"

"I know who you are, too, lady. And you're trouble, according to A." He threw his arm around Liza and tucked her to his side to walk her out of the alley. Hayley had once dated his brother, then taken advantage of his connections at KCPD to further her career. Oh yeah, Atticus was a lot better off marrying a class act like

Brooke than this conniving piece of work. Hayley Resnick needed to get out of Holden's face. "Ms. Parrish has no comment."

Leaving the stymied reporter behind them, Holden hurried Liza around the corner to the side street where the S.W.A.T. van was parked. He opened the back doors and lifted her onto the back bumper. "Get inside."

Liza paced off the length of the narrow passage between their gear and weapons cache while Holden closed the doors behind them. "I'm tired of being bombarded with questions," she raged. "From KCPD. From my therapist. From you, and now that woman. I can't answer every damn one of them. I'm tired, I'm tired, I'm tired."

"Hey. Hey." Holden caught her flailing arms and pulled her to his chest, holding her tight until the tantrum and frustration had worked their way through her system. With a weary huff of breath, Liza finally relaxed, turning her cheek into his shoulder and leaning against him. The hard plates of the flak vest masked the curves of her figure. But there was plenty of woman to hold on to as she nestled her head beneath his chin. He cupped the back of her head with one hand and slid the other down to the swell of her hips.

Holden feathered his fingers through the silky fringe of hair beneath the cap she wore, breathing in the citrus-like scent of her shampoo and the sharper, medicinal smells that clung to her clothes. He whispered apologies for adding to the barrage of questions that weighed with such pressure on her. Her breathing evened out as he continued to talk, and she snuggled against his throat. "Nobody's going to hurt you in here. Nobody's going to ask you to do anything. You're safe now. It's quiet here. Quiet and safe."

His own erratic pulse and turbulent thoughts had calmed during these few moments of tender stillness. But when she pulled back to free her arms and wind them around his waist and move even closer, his heart rate shifted into a higher gear. The vest was cold and stiff against his chest and stomach, but farther down, where their hips and thighs touched, they were generating an amazing heat. It was impossible not to imagine the conflagration that full-on body contact with this woman would feel like.

"I'm not supposed to like you, Kincaid," she whispered against his collar. "I'm not supposed to even know you."

"I know."

"Did you ever read *Romeo and Juliet?*"

He laughed, and he thought he could feel her cheek plump with a smile. "My mom's an English teacher. Where do you think I got a name like Holden Caulfield Kincaid?"

"Seriously?" She tipped her head back to meet his gaze.

"My brothers are Edward Rochester, Thomas Sawyer and Atticus Finch Kincaid. So yeah, I get that I'm a Montague and you're a Capulet." He released one hand just long enough to pull his S.W.A.T. cap off her head so he could read her expression in the van's shaded interior. "I also get that I like you, too."

Liza's fresh, angelic face—momentarily free of attitude or suspicion—was smiling. "Thanks for the rescue, Romeo."

Those peachy lips were parted in anticipation, and, like a hungry man, Holden couldn't resist. He leaned in, brushed his lips against hers. Her taste was sweeter than he'd imagined. And when she lifted onto her toes to press her lips more firmly against his, the spark of that first kiss was hotter than any embrace he'd ever shared with a woman.

Holden tangled his fingers into that sassy, silky hair and pulled her even closer. Moaning with surprise and absolute approval, he traced the seam of her lips with his tongue and ventured inside to deepen the kiss.

The scrape of metal on metal jarred Holden from the unexpected pleasure of that kiss, reminding him that nothing could come of it—that he was only guaranteeing trouble for them both if something *should* come of it. The outside handle on the van turned, and Liza froze. Holden released her and reluctantly retreated as the back door opened.

Kevin Grove's bulky frame and disgruntled mood filled the opening. Lieutenant Cutler, Dominic and the rest of his team were gathered behind the detective, looking up at them with everything from reproach to amusement. Grove looked from Holden to Liza and back to Holden again. "This isn't what I think it is, is it, Kincaid?"

Feeling more than a little disgruntled himself at the interruption—and at allowing the situation to get so personal in the first place, Holden couldn't keep the sarcasm out of his reply. "If you mean securing the witness? Keeping her away from the press? Then, yeah, that's exactly what I'm doing."

"That's why you…?" Liza's voice faded away and an invisible armor thicker than the S.W.A.T. vest she wore lodged into place. Her hair fanned out in a sexy disarray, as though a man's hands had been in it. But she quickly smoothed each spike back into place. "Thank you for your concern, Officer Kincaid."

"Parrish—"

But she was already pushing him aside and reaching for Grove's hand to help her down from the van. "Mr. Kincaid helped me evade a reporter in the alley behind the clinic. But I'm sure she's gone by now. I'd better get back inside to help pack up supplies."

Holden instinctively moved forward when Grove didn't release Liza's hand. "I can't allow you to go back in there, ma'am," said the gruff detective.

"But I have to help out. We have to get the clinic cleaned tonight, or it won't be safe to bring the animals—"

"No, ma'am." Grove cut her off. "You're done working for today. Lieutenant Cutler? I need your team to escort Ms. Parrish to the back of my car."

Holden jumped down from the van. With a gentle tug on her arm, Grove released her, but she shook off Holden's touch as well. Well, hell. She could misread his motivations and be pissed off at him all she wanted, but Holden wasn't going to let Grove order her around as though she was a suspect instead of a victim. "She didn't do anything wrong. She's not responsible for any of this."

"I'm taking her downtown until we can confirm this wasn't an attempt on her life."

"Is that what you think?"

Grove ignored Liza's question and mirrored Holden's defensive stance. "I'm just like you, Kincaid. I'm trying to keep her safe. Do you have a problem with that?"

Holden held his gaze for as long as he could before the lieutenant could call him on it. "No, sir."

"Good. Cutler?" Grove pushed Liza into the triangle formed by Dom, Trip and Delgado, then jogged ahead to clear the path to his vehicle.

Lieutenant Cutler was only slightly more sympathetic. "Keep it together, big guy. You're no use to me if you're not thinking straight. You're no use to her, either." He tapped the center of Holden's chest. "Now put on a spare vest and let's get Ms. Parrish downtown."

Chapter Six

Mr. Smith sat in his room at the historic Raphael Hotel at the south edge of the Plaza, miles away from the fun he'd had earlier this evening. With the extra pillows plumped at his back, and the cabernet sauvignon breathing on the bedside table, he sorted through the names in his file.

He stopped on the picture of the pretty redhead whose bio said she was 25, but who looked ten years younger with that tomboy haircut and freckles.

Mr. Smith picked up the cell phone in his lap and punched in his employer's number. When the phone picked up, there was no greeting, just, "I have her. Liza Parrish. She's your witness."

"So your plan worked?"

"A S.W.A.T. team escorted her away from the scene." It was proof enough for him that he'd exposed the right woman. "Shall I take care of the situation?"

"Give me twenty-four hours to see if I can find out how much she's told anyone. I'm tired of loose ends on this project. If you don't hear from me by tomorrow night at this time, I'll expect you to eliminate her. All trace of her."

"WHAT DO YOU THINK THEY'RE talking about in there?" Holden sat on the corner of Atticus's desk at the Fourth Precinct office, swirling cold coffee in the bottom of his plastic cup.

Atticus pulled off his glasses and swiveled in his chair to look at the conference room where Liza, Detective Grove, the assistant D.A., Lieutenant Cutler and almost a dozen other officers and civilians had gathered behind closed doors. "After three hours? I'm guessing they're talking strategy. Whether she's a witness who's important enough to warrant moving to a safe house. How viable the threat is against her, and what spin they're going to put on this with the media."

"She needed to be in protective custody six months ago."

Atticus loosened his tie and unbuttoned his collar, a sign of just how long this day had gone on. "I've gotten the sense all along that she's been reluctant to tell Grove everything she knows. Or maybe she just doesn't want to get involved."

A woman who rescued three dogs from the pound? Who wanted to go back inside a clinic where a bomb threat had been called in to help clean up the mess? A woman who charged across the street to confront a man she thought was following her? Who stretched up on tiptoe and deepened a forbidden kiss?

Liza Parrish wasn't afraid to get involved. Not that copper-haired spitfire. There had to be something else going on here. But what?

"Mom was good when you saw her?" Atticus asked.

"What? Yeah." The abrupt change in topic startled Holden from his thoughts. "She was having Uncle Bill over for dinner. Edward showed up, too."

"No kidding. How was he?"

"Sober. Healthy." Holden shrugged, suspecting that this tangent in the conversation was his brother's efforts to distract him from worrying about Liza—and feeling guilty that she'd misread his interest in her as some kind of manipulation regarding their father's murder. But with nothing but a closed door to study, he went along with the conversation. "I picked a fight with Edward."

"Really? And how did that work out for you?"

Holden grinned. "Turned out to be kind of a good talk, I think. He was getting rid of Cara and Melinda's things, said he couldn't move on as long as they were around. I suggested he keep a few sentimental items— that he might want them back some day."

"You tried to stop him and he didn't slug you?"

"Not this time. I doubt I'm on his favorite brother list right now, but he stayed to have dinner with Mom and Bill when I got the call to the animal clinic."

A third voice, deep and rumbly, joined the discussion. "Maybe Ed's starting to heal a little bit." Their second oldest brother, Sawyer, came over from his desk where he'd been working at the computer. "At least he's keeping his head above water and coping with the real world— not like he was a year ago." He tossed a print-out onto Atticus's desk. "Take a look at this. I got a hit on that Trent Jameson guy Grove called in. He's a psychologist, known for his groundbreaking research into hypnotherapy."

Atticus picked up the print-out and photo. "Looks like we're in the wrong line of work, boys. Dr. Jameson earns upwards of $10,000 an hour to talk about his research."

Holden scanned the paper next, zeroing in on three lines near the bottom. "This says Dr. Jameson has been sued for malpractice twice in California."

Sawyer leaned across the desk and pointed out the next two lines. "One case was dismissed, the other settled out of court. Psychology isn't a finite science." Sawyer would know, as he continued to go to counseling sessions with his wife, who'd barely survived an abusive first marriage. "Sometimes, a patient has unrealistic expectations about what can be accomplished or how fast it can be done."

"And sometimes, the psychologist just doesn't get the job done." Holden dropped the paper and stood. He tossed his coffee cup into the trash and circled around to stand beside Sawyer—one of the few men in KCPD who stood even taller than he did. "Why the hell would you need a hypnotherapist on a police investigation? If he's there for Liza, anything she'd say under that kind of influence would be inadmissible in court."

Atticus, ever the voice of reason in the family, had a theory. "Could be he's just her regular therapist. We know she doesn't have any family—that they died during a home invasion down at the Lake of the Ozarks a few years back. That's public record. Maybe Jameson is who she calls when she needs a friend around."

Holden knew from their own limited investigation that Liza lived alone and had no parents. But he hadn't realized they'd been murdered. Earlier, at the clinic, she'd asked him how he dealt with all the violence in his line of work. She wasn't just talking about today's events, or even his father's murder. Maybe Liza had seen all the violence she could stand, and Dr. Jameson was helping her cope with that. Could be that, as much as she was willing to work with KCPD, it was just an extremely difficult task for her to get through.

Now all those people were in there, bombarding her with questions?

And she was alone with them?

"Um, where are you going?" Sawyer called after him.

Holden was already halfway to the conference room. He wanted to know if Liza was okay. If Trent Jameson was there to help her. He wanted to know if she'd accept his apology and let her know that, in a room full of Montagues, he was there for his lady Juliet.

He knocked on the door and heard a responding lull in the conversation on the other side. When the heated sounds picked up again as if his interruption was of no consequence, Holden raised his fist to knock again.

The door swung open and Kevin Grove answered. "What do you want? Didn't Cutler dismiss you?"

There were files out on the conference table, a city map had been pinned to the wall. A least three different conversations were going on at once.

"Kincaid?" Holden looked past Grove's shoulder and zeroed in on Liza's tight-lipped expression. Her eyes locked on to his.

"You okay?" Holden didn't know if he'd whispered or shouted.

But his words reached their target. Her slight nod would have been more convincing if her skin wasn't so pale and her hands weren't clenched into fists on top of the table. Dr. Jameson, who sat beside her, patted her arm, demanding her attention. She glanced at the doctor for a moment, then swung her gaze back to Holden.

"I'm sorry about all this."

Grove was the only one who heard his apology as he urged Holden back into the main room and closed the door behind him. "Sorry, pal, you're not invited to the party."

"What are you doing to her in there?"

"Go home." Grove's tone was sympathetic enough,

but he wasn't budging from the doorway. "You've done your job with Miss Parrish. Now let me do mine."

For a split second, Holden debated whether he could shove the burly ogre aside. Given his current mood, he probably could get past him. But the thought of fighting his way through all the rest of the officers inside—as well as a little common sense and departmental protocol—made him think that walking away was a better choice. For now.

Ignoring the questions and unwanted advice from his brothers, Holden stalked down the hallway to the men's room. He took care of business then went to the sink to splash cold water on his face.

When he straightened, he looked into the mirror and saw he had company.

Kevin Grove turned on a spigot two sinks down and washed his hands.

Holden took his time drying his. This meeting wasn't a coincidence.

When Grove reached for the paper towels, he finally spoke. "Anything you want to tell me about you and Liza Parrish?" Holden wadded his towel and tossed it without answering. "Don't pretend you don't know her. I saw Hayley Resnick's news report. And I know what a bodyguard looks like."

"Liza needs one."

"It shouldn't be you." Grove pitched his trash and buttoned his suit jacket. "You two have history?"

About seventy-two hours worth.

But the connection to Liza Parrish was there, and he wasn't going to deny it. "I want in. Even if I'm just the runner who delivers the pizza and bagels to the safe house you're sticking her in, I want to be on her protection detail."

Grove seemed to give his request real consideration. "I don't like it. But if you want to help, you may get your wish. Come with me."

Holden shrugged at his brothers' curious expressions as he followed Kevin Grove into the conference room. Some sort of decision must have been reached because folders were now closed, and at least one of the conversations he overheard was about a new truck someone was thinking about buying.

Grove waved Liza over, but she was already on her feet and hurrying around the table.

"Thank you." She beamed a smile up at him that elicited half a grin of his own.

But he was still missing something here. "Thank me for what?"

Liza pulled back the lab coat she still wore and reached into the front pocket of her jeans.

Grove started to fill in the blanks. "Miss Parrish won't even talk about cooperating with us until she knows her dogs are okay."

Well, hell.

She pulled a key ring from her pocket, then proceeded to remove what looked like a house key. "Bruiser, Cruiser and Yukon have been locked up in the house all day long. They need to be fed again, given fresh water and taken out for their run. Otherwise, I'm afraid they'll chew up my couch or leave some unexpected presents for me."

"That's what you want me to do? You want me to check on the damn dogs?"

Liza tucked the extra keys back in her jeans, looking

a bit stunned by his response. She glanced up at Grove, then propped her hands at her hips and turned on the attitude. "Would you excuse us for a minute, detective?"

With a reluctant nod, Grove stepped aside and Liza nudged Holden out the door. He got around the corner into a secluded hallway before the attack started. "Look, Kincaid—those dogs are my family, and I'm responsible for them. I'm just asking you to do a favor."

Holden could go on the offensive, too. He backed her toward the wall. "I'm a trained special weapons and tactics officer. I've taken survivalist training and I know how a man like the guy who's after you thinks. And you want me to let your dogs out?" When he realized he was venting more frustrated emotion than cool-headed logic, he retreated a step and softened his voice to a more rational tone. "Is this some kind of punishment for kissing you?"

"No. I—"

"Because I wanted to. And if it wouldn't cost me my badge, I'd do it again."

"You want to kiss me again?"

"Like hell on fire."

The freckles vanished as a blush colored her cheeks. Her gaze fell to the center of his chest, possibly to the badge hanging on a chain there. "Could you really lose your job by getting involved with me?"

His chest expanded with a deep sigh. "I'd at least get a reprimand in my file. Maybe get a promotion delayed. But I didn't want you to get into trouble, either. I want you to be focused on your testimony and help find justice for my dad. And I want you to listen to the men who are in there trying to figure out how to protect you."

She reached out and touched his badge, gently,

almost reverently. "You look just like your dad, you know. The first time I saw you—for a second, I thought I was looking at a ghost." She pulled her hand away. "You've been through so much already. I don't want to get you into trouble. I'm sorry. I won't bother asking you for the favor."

When she turned to walk away, Holden's heart nearly imploded inside his chest. He snatched her hand and pulled it back to his chest, splaying her fingers over his aching heart and holding them there.

Shakespeare wasn't the only one who could create a mess with an unwise but irresistible relationship. "Talk to me about the dogs."

"I need someone to take care of them." The warmth of her hand and the growing brightness of her smile seemed to have a healing effect on his ravaged conscience. "They know you. At least, out of all the choices in that room, you're the only one the dogs have met. Cruiser definitely has a crush on you. And Bruiser will like anybody who gives him treats. And Yukon, well... he needs someone with a strong will and a commanding voice in order to stay in line."

She paused unexpectedly, turning her head to the side. Holden tucked two fingers beneath her chin and turned her face back to his. "A commanding voice I can do. What else?"

"I need someone to understand what those dogs mean to me, Kincaid. I owe those three everything. They're the only thing I have in my life that I can always count on."

Holden looked down at those beseeching gray eyes that wanted so badly to trust. He released her hand and reached for the one that still held the key. He caught both the key and her fingers and held on tight. And he made a vow.

"No, they're not."

Chapter Seven

Liza decided that Kevin Grove was a lot nicer than his gruff demeanor first led her to believe. She wouldn't make the mistake of thinking he had changed his mind about needing her testimony to nail John Kincaid's killer—after all, he'd stationed police officers in unmarked vehicles at either end of her block, and had ordered two more on foot to patrol the wooded area behind her house. But she'd discovered that he could put that bulldog tenacity on hold and actually be a bit of a softy—for short periods of time, at any rate.

"All right," he groused, apparently satisfied with all the electronic sensors and listening devices he'd plugged into her telephone and set up around each door and window of her house. "I'm going out on the porch to uh, have a cigarette." His expression was far less amenable when he looked over at Holden, lounging against the kitchen sink. "You can have that long with her before I chase you out tonight."

"You don't smoke," Holden pointed out.

"Do you want me to step outside or not?"

"Enjoy your break, detective."

Once they were the last two people in the house, Liza

pushed Bruiser's head off her lap and got up from the kitchen table to rinse the milk from her empty glass. Her brownies had been a hit with each of the security team members who'd come inside, and she pulled the now-empty baking dish off the counter and scooted Holden aside while she filled it with water to soak overnight.

While she'd been dutifully listening to every security precaution that Grove had insisted upon, Holden had been out on the exercise path with the three musketeers, as he'd dubbed her menagerie of pets. "So how did your evening go?"

"Great. Everyone's been run, fed, watered, and now they're settling down to sleep it off." He nodded toward Bruiser, who was still circling the table, looking for something edible fall to his level. "Except for Mooch-face over there. You'd think he'd be full by now."

Liza laughed, and the black and tan terrier mix took the sound as an invitation and trotted across the linoleum to join them. "This one's never full. Probably comes from living on the streets and eating food whenever and wherever he could find it."

Holden rinsed the empty glass he'd been drinking from and put it in the sink beside hers. "You said Bruiser's the dog you were rescuing the night you found Dad?"

She nodded. "Bruiser was skin and bones when I found him under a Dumpster in that alley. You could see every rib, each hip bone—his nails were overgrown and he could barely stand on his own when I picked him up." Liza smothered a sob at the sad irony of her situation. Details about the dog she could remember. But details about the gunshots and the men who'd killed Holden's father?

"Hey." A strong, gentle finger twisted through a wisp of hair at her temple and tucked it behind her ear. "Don't go there. Not tonight. You've had enough to deal with already today."

"Thank you."

"For what? Not pushing? Not tonight."

When he leaned in like that, she could see that Holden really did have long eyelashes. The beauty of them was so at odds with the ruggedly masculine angles of his face that it made noticing them feel like she'd discovered a secret about him. One that was hers alone to keep. "I'm sorry you've been reduced to dog-sitter, but trust me, from my perspective, you're the hero of the day."

"Just doin' my job, ma'am," he drawled in that soothing, warming pitch.

She tore her gaze away from his blue eyes and found herself staring, for the second time that night, at the brass and blue enamel badge that hung around his neck. He was a cop, just like his father. Just like each of his brothers, apparently. Watching Holden and his S.W.A.T. teammates work and joke with each other, seeing Detective Grove's diligence and the dedication of each of the officers who'd been in that conference room with her earlier tonight, she was beginning to understand that there was a brotherhood among the members of the KCPD that went beyond badges and bloodlines.

One of their own had been murdered. And they were all looking to her to give them the answers they needed to bring their brother's—or father's—killer to justice. The weight of that responsibility was daunting. But she vowed tonight, more than ever, that she would do whatever was necessary to restore her memories and give them the answers they—and she—needed.

But standing close to Holden like this, in the warmth

of her kitchen, with his fingers stroking gently at her temple, and his seductive voice calming her more effectively than any therapy or medication, Liza began to believe that she *would* remember what she needed to one day. With every breath of his clean, undoctored scent, made musky by the work of the day, Liza began to believe that she wasn't quite so alone in the world. As unbelievable as it seemed, in the short few days that she'd known Holden Kincaid, she was beginning to think that she might be falling in love with him. Could reality be working as quickly as Shakespearean fiction?

"You tired?" he asked, misreading her silence and pulling away.

"Exhausted." She summoned a smile to alleviate his concern. She was in no way, shape or form ready to admit to her thoughts. "But then I'm a grad student doing her internship, so I'm pretty much always tired."

"Then I'd better be saying good-night so you can get to bed. Make sure Grove sleeps on the couch, okay?"

"If the dogs let him." Not quite ready to let Holden's reassuring presence go, she started plucking short, tawny hairs off his black uniform shirt. "I can see from the evidence here that you were playing with Cruiser. I told you she's got a crush on you."

"Yeah, I've always been popular with the ladies." Liza arched an eyebrow at the macho bravado in his voice. "By the way, the little guy likes me, too."

Liza scooped up Bruiser and cradled the dog high in her arms, holding him so that he could rest his front paws on Holden's chest. "Do you like Kincaid, too, Bruiser?" In answer, the dog licked Holden's face. "Oh, yes, you do. Yes, you do."

"Easy, tough guy." Holden smiled wryly, grabbed

the dog's muzzle in a playful grip and pushed his tongue away. "Not exactly the kiss I was hoping for."

Laughing in a way she hadn't for a long time, Liza pulled Bruiser down to her hip and reached up to wipe the traces of the dog's lick off Holden's cheek. His eyes locked on to hers at the caress, and the piercing blue color warmed, warming her in turn. Sliding her hand around to the sandy-brown crop of hair above his starched collar, Liza pulled his head down to hers. *This* was the kiss she wanted him to have. The kiss she wanted to receive.

Holden's hands came up to frame her face and feather into her hair as his mouth opened, moist and deliberate, over hers. She parted her lips and his tongue swept in, as familiar and wonderful as if they'd kissed like this before. Liza whimpered at the delicious tingling that danced through her blood when she slid her tongue against his.

Making a basket with his fingers, Holden tilted her head back and closed the distance between them, plundering her mouth with a lazy thoroughness that made her breathing erratic and her breasts heavy with need. She stroked her palm over the sandpapery stubble at his jaw, then let her hand trail over the soft knit turtleneck at the column of his throat. He claimed everything she was willing to give, stamping his touch, his healing, his passion onto her eager mouth.

Liza's fingers slipped lower, hooking on a button and unfastening it. She slid her hand inside his shirt, rubbing her palm over the ridges of his sweater and squeezing her fingertips into the warmer bulge of muscle underneath.

Holden's hands were moving, too. He dragged them

down along her spine, creating a heated friction that warmed her from her skin to her core. When he reached her hips, his fingers spread downward, catching the curve of her bottom through her jeans and lifting her into his growing arousal. Pulling her closer. Kissing her harder.

An icy cold nose poked her chin, startling Liza. With a gasp, she drew away.

"Bruiser! Oh." A different kind of heat flooded her cheeks and left her feeling slightly unbalanced. She set the dog on the floor and sucked in a couple of deep breaths, trying to clear her head and ready an apology for spoiling the passionate moment. "Sorry about that." She shot her fingers through her hair and glared at the innocent pooch. "I can't believe I forgot we had company."

But Holden was smiling instead of complaining. "Don't apologize. I kind of lost track of where I was myself. That kiss was perfect." He touched her lips. They felt swollen and hot, and they chased after Holden's fingers as he grinned and pulled them away. "Perfect."

It was only when he reached up to rebutton his shirt that she saw his hands quaking with the same kind of tremors that seemed to be dissipating like aftershocks through her body. "I'd better go before Grove comes back in and arrests me for loitering."

Liza walked him to the front door. She could definitely see the dangers of things moving so quickly between them. Romeo and Juliet had acted impulsively on their ill-conceived passion, and look where it had gotten them. Still, Liza had felt more secure, more herself, more alive in these few hours she'd spent with Holden Kincaid than she'd felt since before her parents' deaths. As heady as it was frightening, it wasn't a feeling she was eager to let go. "Will you be back tomorrow?"

"Nobody can keep me away." He stopped at the door and looked behind her to the furry trio making themselves comfortable on and around her couch. "After all, I promised the three musketeers that I'd take them for a run in the morning." His gaze came back to her upturned face. "And we'd hate to disappoint them."

"We sure would."

"Plus, if you're going to thank me like that every night…" He let the invitation, the promise, linger in the air.

He dipped his head and caught her mouth in a quick kiss—a graphic, vibrant, all-too-brief reminder of the passion they'd just shared. "Until tomorrow morning."

"Good night, Kincaid."

He knocked to signal Grove that he was coming out before opening the door.

"Good night… Liza."

"I AM NOT GOING WITHOUT MY DOGS. Period. End of discussion."

Holden stood back like a fly on the wall while Kevin Grove and Lieutenant Cutler tried to argue with Liza about the benefits of moving her to a more secure safe house. He'd shown up at about seven in his sweats and running shoes to find Liza practically stomping around her kitchen, feeding the dogs and the cops breakfast and filling the dishwasher while zipping back to take periodic glances at a thick textbook which lay open on the table. Her hair was still damp from a shower and drying naturally into chunky wisps that she occasionally smoothed with her fingers.

The woman was a dynamo of energy, and Grove and Cutler didn't stand a chance.

"I thought you'd arranged everything so that I could stay here," she went on, jotting something from the text onto a note card and sticking it into the back pocket of her jeans.

Kevin Grove looked like he needed sleep more than he needed the mug of coffee he cradled in his hands. "That was before you told us about the car nearly running you down night before last. If someone has already IDed your house and is following you, then we'd like to throw him off the trail by putting you up someplace where he can't look up your address in a phone book."

She shooed Bruiser away from the open dishwasher, added soap to the dispenser and then started the machine. "I told you, I'm perfectly willing to cooperate as long as you move me someplace that can house them, too."

"The dogs complicate things." Cutler tried to explain one of the lessons of witness protection Holden had been taught. "They require going in and out—"

"*I* require going in and out."

"Three dogs would draw attention to the house. The idea is to blend in with the scenery so no one suspects what kind of operation is going on inside."

Holden scratched Cruiser's smooth head as the greyhound leaned against his leg and thrust her head into his hand. They could throw out logical appeals until they were blue in the face, but Holden was quickly learning that arguing with Liza Parrish with her mind made up was like arguing with a brick wall. Cutler and Grove should give up now. They had a better chance of being hit by lightning than of separating Liza from her pets.

"Why can't you just post more guards here at my house?" Liza picked up her backpack from beside her chair, closed the book and stuffed it inside.

"We have a budget to consider—"

"Would you stay put inside?"

"No." Liza zipped the bag shut and plopped it back on the floor. "I have classes to attend, a job to go to."

Cutler leaned back in his chair. "Not for a few days, you don't. You wouldn't want to put any of your classmates or coworkers at risk, do you?"

"No."

Holden straightened away from the wall as Liza sank into her chair at the table. Cutler had used a hostage negotiation technique on her, and it had worked. Liza was thinking about worst-case scenarios now, evaluating how her choices could affect the people she cared about.

"What about my appointments with Dr. Jameson?" With a little less zing in her voice, she turned her argument to Kevin Grove. "You said they were more important now than ever. I'm supposed to see him this morning."

"He can come here."

"Trent Jameson?" Sitting didn't last very long for Liza. She was up out of her chair, pacing the length of her kitchen as she continued. "Do you know what kind of convincing it took to get him to come down to the police station last night?"

Grove carried his coffee mug to the sink and rinsed it out. "Jameson is a citizen of the community who can do his public duty like the rest of us and work here for one day. The city will still pay him his basic fee, whether he does the job at his office or here."

"The city's paying Jameson ten thousand dollars to counsel you?" The words were out before Holden could stop them. "What about the department's shrink that you told me to go to?"

Liza's arms slid around her waist in a self-comforting

hug that he wished he could give her. Her gaze slid toward the corner of the room where Holden stood, but didn't quite reach his eyes. What the hell was going on here?

Lieutenant Cutler pushed away from the table and stood. "I recommended our psychologist to you because I just needed you to blow off some steam and focus. What I understand from our meeting last night is that Miss Parrish is part of some kind of research study." He glanced at Grove and Liza to verify his explanation. "Apparently, Dr. Jameson has developed a treatment program that works specifically with witnesses like her."

Liza nodded. But Holden still felt as though he was missing something when she continued to avoid eye contact. "Dr. Jameson wasn't particularly pleased with the results of my session at the precinct offices. He thinks I'll do better in the controlled space of his office," she said. "There would be too many people, too many distractions here."

"Fine," Grove agreed. "We'll escort you to Jameson's for your appointment."

"Before we go, can I go for a run with my dogs? I'm not used to sitting around so much. They aren't, either."

"Should I just paint a 'Shoot me' sign on your back?" Holden moved forward. "You're out of line, Grove."

"Back off, Kincaid."

Cutler positioned himself between the two men. "Boys!"

Liza tried to be a little more reasonable. "Presidents of the United States have gone running with their Secret Service men. Why don't you all just come with me?"

"I'll go with her," Holden volunteered. Her pent-up energy pushed against the walls of the house. Like Cutler had told him, she needed to blow off some steam if KCPD wanted her to keep her head in the game. "Trip, Molloy and Delgado can come, too. We have to do daily fitness training, anyway. We could take care of both jobs at the same time."

Cutler nodded. "Fine."

"Cutler!" Kevin Grove's protest boomed through the house, startling Cruiser and sending her trotting out of the kitchen. "Miss Parrish is *my* responsibility. This is my—"

"The investigation may be yours. But security is my detail. She's fighting us on things the way they are, so if we give on this, we'll get more cooperation in return. I trained these men myself. I guarantee you they'll keep her safe." He turned and dismissed Holden with a nod. "I want her in a vest, and I want your team armed and hooked up to a radio at all times."

"Yes, sir."

Resisting the urge to gloat, Holden opened his phone and crossed into the living room to call Dominic and the others. After hanging up on Delgado a few minutes later, Holden tuned in to the hushed voices of the two men still arguing in the kitchen. Liza was still in her bedroom changing.

"If this doesn't pan out, I can't make my case. This better be worth the trouble we're going to for this witness."

"Is there any reason why it wouldn't be?" Cutler asked.

"I kept her name out of the press for as long as I could. Now that the world knows we've got a witness to John Kincaid's murder, the bastards behind his death will be closing in. The clock is ticking." Kevin Grove's curse drew Holden closer to the archway to eavesdrop. "I just hope she remembers what she needs to before they get through us and find her."

"They won't get through—"

"Remember what she needs to?" Holden had never been one to avoid a confrontation when something needed to be said. He stepped into the kitchen and demanded an explanation. "What does that mean?"

Grove scowled, looking even more like a bulldog than ever, then he laughed. "You mean with all the un-sanctioned snooping you and your brothers have been doing for the past six months, you don't know?"

"Don't know what?"

"Your girlfriend didn't tell you?"

"Grove…"

"Allow me, detective."

Holden turned at Liza's voice.

She stood in the kitchen archway, pulling a navy blue sweatshirt down over her gray, fitted running suit. She tilted her chin up proudly, defensively—but the robust energy that had sparkled in her eyes a few minutes ago had vanished.

"I'm sorry, Kincaid. I want to help your family and KCPD, I really do." Something inside him sagged as her own deep sigh rounded her shoulders. But she never once lowered her gaze. "I suffer from traumatic amne-sia. I remember finding Bruiser, and I remember finding your father. But what happened in between? All I know is I was afraid. I can't tell you who murdered your father…because I don't remember."

LIZA JUMPED INSIDE HER skin as two gunshots exploded in the night.

"Relax. You're perfectly safe here." She wasn't sure she believed Dr. Jameson, but she tried to obey. "Breathe deeply, Liza. Return to your quiet place."

She hugged the pillow to her stomach and focused on her breathing.

Liza clutched the emaciated dog tightly in her arms and smelled the dank river. The sound of tires on the damp pavement drew her attention to the front of the alley. She muzzled the dog with her hand and crouched down low, flattening her back against the rough brick wall. Car doors slammed and she could hear men's voices. One of them laughed.

"Liza?" Dr. Jameson's voice filtered into her mind. "I need you to tell me what you're seeing. What you hear."

The spring night was damp this close to the river. The moisture of it clung to the dog's fur and intensified his sour smell. Thank goodness she'd parked far away, because the men wouldn't realize she was here. Of course, she hadn't known how far she'd have to go to track down this dog Anita had told her about. She hadn't known she'd be witnessing a murder.

"Liza." His tone was a little sharper now, less patient than the gentle voice that had lulled her into this sleepy state. "Can you hear my voice?"

She nodded. "I hear you."

"Good." The soft music in the room was replaced with the abrasive whine of a rusty metal door sliding open. Someone was coming out of the warehouse. Or was someone going in? She couldn't see. "Now I want to you move closer to the black car. Open the door in your mind and tell me what you see."

She pulled her mind back to the car, to the images she could barely see. "Two men. One has white hair and tattoos clear around his neck and down his arms. He isn't wearing a coat."

"Good. What does the other man look like?"

She peered through a gap between the plastic bags. The stench of the rotting garbage inside made her eyes tear up and her nose run.

"Tell me about the other man."

"He's—"

Liza's mind shuttered, as if someone had drawn a blindfold over her eyes. There was only blackness inside her head. "Doctor…?"

"Relax. Breathe deeply. In through your nose, out…"

Dr. Jameson's words got lost in the fog of her memory. Another voice—cold, heartless—shivered down her spine. *"Did you hear that?"*

The skinny dog could barely move, but he still had fight in him. His mournful whine vibrated through his body and echoed along the walls of the alley.

Fresh tears stung Liza's eyes, replacing the caustic irritation of the garbage with the shock of bone-deep fear. She stroked her fingers along the dog's empty, distended belly, desperately coaxing him into silence.

"Tell me about the other man, Liza. Who's there with you?"

"It's just a mutt." The tattooed man's voice was higher in pitch than the other man's. *"I had a dog when I was a kid. I lived in Yugoslavia back then. Hell, they don't even have Yugoslavia anymore. I miss that dog."*

"I hate dogs."

The other man sounded vaguely familiar. But how could it? She'd never been to this part of Kansas City before. She didn't know these men.

"What is it, Liza?" Dr. Jameson kept pushing. "Tell me what you're seeing."

"From the sound of it, he'll be dead by morning."

"If someone hears it, they may call the police."

"*Or the dog catcher.*" *The tattooed man laughed.*
"*Do they still have dog catchers?*"

"*If anyone comes, it could give us away before the boss is finished with the mission.*" *There was a rasp and a click that Liza couldn't identify.*

"*What are you gonna do with that gun?*"

"*I'm going to track down that dog and shut him up.*"

Liza jerked as if she'd been slapped. Suddenly, she was in a different place. At a different time. "No. Please. I don't want to be here."

"*From the look of things, the dog was probably trying to defend the place when they broke in.*" *The police woman who'd called Liza home from college was trying to be kind.*

"*I'm sure Shasta barked at the intruders.*"

"*Then I imagine they did it to shut her up. Before the neighbors could hear. She was the one alarm they couldn't shut off with a stolen key code.*"

So the thieves had shot her dog.

"No. Mom? Dad?" They'd killed her dog. Killed her parents. Liza was locked inside her head with the nightmare. The hot tears that leaked from beneath the silk eye mask were as real as the pain she felt. "I don't want to do this anymore." Was she speaking out loud? Was she dreaming? "Make it stop. Mom and Dad are dead. I don't want to see that again."

"Damn it, Liza. Go back to the alley."

Her jumbled up mind struggled to sort out the present and the past.

"Test subject is too agitated to remain in deep suggestive state." Dr. Jameson was talking into his recorder. "Drug therapy is only recourse left to pursue."

Her parents' deaths were in the past.

Men who would murder were in the past.

"Liza, I'm going to count to three and you will be awake. One…"

"I don't want to do this," she pleaded.

"Two…"

Drug therapy?

"Three."

Liza's eyes popped open beneath the mask. She ripped it off her face and squinted up at the ceiling, waiting for the ivy-print border to come into focus. When the rapid rise and fall of her chest evened out and she thought she could sit up without the room spinning around her head, she did. The headache wasn't as bad this time, just a dull twinge behind her eyes. But the fear and confusion were more disconcerting than ever. "Dr. Jameson, I don't think this is helping."

He looked up from the notes he'd been scribbling. "You're too impatient. You don't listen to me half the time. It's no wonder we can't make this work."

"I'm not taking drugs. I heard you say that. Even for the truth, I won't do it."

With a scoffing noise, he tossed off his reading glasses and went to his desk to turn on a lamp. "I'm only talking about a small dose of Sodium Penthothal to relax you."

"Truth serum?" Hadn't she already surrendered enough control of her mind to this man? She wasn't about to turn what was left of it over to some drug. "Like they use to get POWs to talk? No, thanks."

"You watch too much television."

"Not much at all, really." She grabbed her backpack and slung it over her shoulder as she stood up. Holden and two of the members of his S.W.A.T. team were waiting for her out in the reception area. A fourth member was parked out front in their armored van. It would be damn near impossible to talk them into taking her somewhere besides straight home, but she intended to try. Being locked up inside her home with Holden's brooding silences, now that he knew she wasn't able to help him solve his father's murder, after all, sounded about as appealing as Trent Jameson's plan to inject her with drugs. "I need some fresh air."

"Where do you think you're going?"

"We're done, right?" She gestured toward the closed shades at the window. "I need sunlight and the smell of the leaves on the ground. I can't be cooped up in here or inside my head for another minute."

Jameson moved fast for a man more than twice her age. When Liza opened his office door, he was suddenly there, reaching over her shoulder and slamming it shut. "What aren't you telling me?"

A momentary burst of fear stuttered through her next breath, but Liza quickly replaced the panic with her mouthy, street-savvy attitude. "We're done here."

"Liza?" Holden's voice was a distant call.

"We are done when I say we're done." Jameson grasped her arm and spun her around, forcing her to read the disappointment and accusation etched on his face. "You've been fighting against me from our very first session. My therapeutic techniques have been proven successful by other patients. Why are you working against me?"

Liza shrugged off his touch and shrank against the door. "It's nothing personal. What the hell kind of doctor are you?"

"I'm the kind who gets results. When my patients cooperate."

There was some kind of commotion in the outer office. "Liza?"

"Officer, I can't let you… He's with a patient."

"Step aside, lady."

Liza wished she was on the other side of this door to see it. "Well, I'm not one of your patients anymore."

Liza reached behind her to turn the knob, but Jameson slapped his hand against the wood beside her head. "*You* have no idea what you're up against, do you. Someone murdered someone else, and they think you know who they are—"

A familiar jolt of fear, just as powerful as anything she'd felt in that dark alley, made her heart pump faster. "I want out of here. Now."

"—and whether you ever remember them or not, they're going to want you dead."

"Liza!"

Jameson pulled her away from the door as the knob turned from the other side. The door flew open, tearing the wood beneath its hinges.

Liza saw the gun pointing at Dr. Jameson before she felt the hand clamp down over her arm and drag her behind the wall of Holden's back. "Are you hurt?"

"No. But I want to leave. He wouldn't let me leave."

"We can fix that."

She was staring at a sea of black. No, she was surrounded by a shield of crisp black uniforms as the slow-talking Trip and raven-haired Dominic Molloy took up flanking positions a step behind Holden. Their guns weren't drawn, but they each rested their hand on the gun butt sticking out from their holsters. One kept an eye on the receptionist, the other had a hand on Holden's back, guiding him so he could back out of

Jameson's office without taking his eye—or his gun—off the doctor.

Jameson seemed unimpressed with the efficient show of force. "You'll pay for this door, I'm assuming?"

"Go to hell."

Liza curled her fingers around Holden's belt, unsure whether she was holding on for her own safety or urging him to retreat. "Please, Kincaid."

Holden held his stance a moment longer before he turned in a fluid ripple of motion, took her by the arm again and steered her past the receptionist's desk toward the outer door and the elevators at the end of the hallway. "We're out of here. Dom, take point. Trip—"

"Don't worry, the doctor will stay right where he is."

Trip could block Jameson in his office, but he couldn't stop the therapist from calling after her. "I know your nightmares torment you, Liza. You think that if you could just remember everything the police want you to that you could put them out of your mind. It's that searching for answers, for closure, that keeps the nightmares coming back. You know I'm your best chance to unlock those hidden places inside your head. You'll never find peace without me. You know that. You'll come back to me."

Every taunt was a cruel "I told you so" that hit its mark and left Liza clutching the rail at the back of the elevator and sagging against it.

"You shut the hell up, doc," Holden ordered. "The lady's done with you."

Liza perked up at the protective anger in his tone as the door slid shut. She wanted Holden to turn around and take her into his arms, to let her feel—and not just hear—that he was still on her side, that his disappointment at her inability to help with the case hadn't completely eroded the connection growing between them. But he was snapping orders into the radio at this shoulder, ordering Delgado to have the van in place when they walked out the front doors.

He was cold and remote, like a machine, and seemed not at all interested in offering comfort to a woman who'd kept the truth from him and his family.

"What was that about?" Molloy asked, apparently less affected by the tension of the situation than Holden was.

"Desperation," Liza answered, when no one else spoke. "Maybe we can get Hayley Resnick to broadcast that my brain is mush and that there's no sense in the bad guys coming after me because I don't know who they are." The joke was lame and nobody laughed. The headache behind Liza's eyes deepened to a throb as tears burned in her sinuses and threatened to spill over again. Riding down seven floors, staring at the center of Holden's broad back, was cruelly symbolic of the bleak turn her life had taken. She'd ceased to be useful to him, but he was still determined to do his job, to protect her even though he now probably thought it was a waste of time. Maybe he even thought that the feelings he had for her were a waste of time. "I'm sorry, Kincaid. I really thought Dr. Jameson could help me remember."

"He's not interested in justice. From the look of things, Jameson was using you like a lab rat to further his own career." That almost musical warmth that she'd found so soothing in Holden's voice had returned, though he never turned around or relaxed his guarded posture. But at least he was talking to her again. That was a good thing, right? "You don't need to go back there."

"What if I can't remember on my own?"

"Then I guess I'll have to find another way to find who killed my father."

MR. SMITH TURNED OFF THE tape recorder, pulled out the tape and crushed the plastic cassette in his leather-gloved fist. He tossed it on the floor next to Trent Jameson's body and pulled his cell phone from his belt.

He punched in his employer's number as he paged through Jameson's treatise on "Hypnotherapy Applications to Memory Recovery Technique." Looked like the good doctor was puffed up on his own ego and liked to hear himself talk. According to his research here, he'd had success with "Scent Triggers" and "Guided Recall" with some of his patients. But when it came to Liza Parrish…

His employer picked up the call.

"I don't think she knows enough to put us away," Mr. Smith reported.

"How certain are we that she'll never remember the details of the crime?"

Mr. Smith didn't need Jameson's therapy to remember the information he'd read in his files. "It's fifty-fifty. But chances are, since it's trauma and not injury-induced, she will, one day, remember. Could be tomorrow, could be when she's ninety-two." He closed the treatise and rose from behind Jameson's desk. "How do you want me to proceed?"

"Even when she's ninety-two, the statute of limitations won't have run out on Kincaid's murder. He was a thorn in my side for thirty years while he was alive. It's not fair that he should continue to haunt me now that he's dead."

Striding past the receptionist slumped over her desk,

Mr. Smith turned out the lights and closed the door behind him. He pushed the button for the elevator and waited for a reply.

With a bastion of KCPD officers shadowing Liza Parrish 24/7 now, he needed to move quickly or this could get messy. He could handle messy, but clean and swift was so much easier.

"I need you to give me the order."

This time, his employer didn't hesitate.

"Kill her."

Chapter Eight

Holden finished toweling off and pulled on his shorts and camo pants before rummaging through the duffel bag. He felt out of place, like an intruder himself, showering in Liza's bathroom, with its blue border of Noah's ark and animals circling the ceiling, and a collection of plastic and ceramic animal pairs sitting on the shelves above the toilet and towel racks.

Probably not the most apt place to unpack the spare hunting clothes he kept in the back of his Mustang for impromptu weekend getaways. It was a habit he'd learned from his dad. There'd been hundreds of times growing up—and as a man—that he and his dad, one or all his brothers and often Bill Caldwell, had kissed Susan Kincaid goodbye and gone off to hunt or fish, or simply camp and enjoy the outdoors. The eyes of every cute little critter seemed to be watching him, judging him. At least he'd left his Bushmaster rifle stowed in the trunk.

He opened the velcro pocket where he'd stored his service Glock, and looped the holster onto his belt, along with his badge.

The irony of who he was, and who Liza seemed to

be—his Montague to her Capulet—only added to the guilt he carried on his shoulders.

He had a thing for the copper-haired animal lover. Maybe he'd let his lust for her impair his judgment. But hell, it was more than that; their connection had been sealed the first time their eyes met across the crowded precinct floor. He'd known something wasn't kosher about all the delays in KCPD's investigation into his father's murder. There had always been something suspicious about an alleged eyewitness whose identity was kept secret. Yet, if she was so valuable a lead, why were only sketchy details on the case being pursued?

Now he understood.

She'd lied to him, damn it. All right, so it was a lie of omission, but neglecting to mention her amnesia was a pretty big lie all the same. She wasn't the key to solving his father's murder, after all. There was no face she could describe or breakthrough clue she could provide. She couldn't tell KCPD any more about his father's murder than the dog she'd rescued that night.

He'd pinned all his hope on her—probably a damn foolish thing for a man his age to do. A trained cop, no less. After knowing her for only a few hours, he'd been so desperate to end the suffering and uncertainty his family was going through that he'd latched on to Liza Parrish as though she was some kind of avenging angel who, if he could just push the right buttons and keep her in one piece, would finally reveal the truth that could give his family closure. She was a scrappy fighter. She had the strength and drive to get the job done.

And he loved her for that.

After four short days, he loved her.

"Ain't that a kick in the pants," he chided his reflection in the fogged-up mirror, before pulling on a clean T-shirt and khaki green sweater.

How could he really love a woman who harbored big secrets he knew nothing about? He was supposed to choose loyalty to his family over his own desires, right?

It had taken overhearing that bizarre, abusive therapy session with Trent Jameson for Holden to get off his pity pot and realize he still had a job to do. His emotions had gotten in the way of clear thinking again, just like they had on that Al Mabry shoot earlier in the week. No matter how conflicted he felt about Liza, nobody deserved to be put through that kind of hell. Nobody.

He just wasn't sure he knew how to get past the betrayal he felt—that he probably had no right to feel. Or maybe it was the disappointment in his own judgment. He didn't trust what might be in his heart any more than he trusted Liza right now.

His life had been a hell of a lot easier when he could ice over his feelings, stop second-guessing his decisions and just do what needed to be done. He missed his father tonight as much as he had the day of his funeral. John Kincaid would have known what to say, how to guide his youngest son through this. He'd probably tell him to grab his fishing pole, pack some food, and they'd go out into the country somewhere. Pitch a tent. Drop their lines in the water. Talk. Listen. And by the time they got back home, Holden would know what to do.

But his father wasn't here to guide him anymore.

Holden squashed the pain of all he had lost into an icy ball inside his chest and let it numb his confusion. He pulled on his socks and hiking boots, packed his muddy sweats in the bag and turned off the light before opening the door. At this time of night, even with the shades drawn, any interior light would give a perp outside a pretty good idea of where there was activity—and a possible target—inside the house.

He slung the duffel bag over his shoulder and walked out into the darkened living room. He'd stop in the kitchen one last time to fill the dogs' water bowls before he left through the side door to the driveway where he'd parked his Mustang. According to Cutler, his only job right now was to guard the dogs. It sucked at Holden's pride to be relegated to glorified dog-walker, but maybe it was the only job he was suited for until he could get his head screwed on straight again.

Kevin Grove was sitting in the lone chair in the living room, holding a flashlight and reading a book, when Holden walked in. Though he couldn't exactly claim that they'd become friends, they had developed a certain rapport that involved an acceptance of their differences, a little respect and a healthy dose of traded barbs.

Holden inclined his head toward the novel by Tolkien in Grove's hands. "Who knew a big lug like you could read. And it's not even a picture book. Impressive." He adjusted his duffel over his shoulder. "Thanks for letting me clean up."

The burly detective bookmarked his page and shut off the light. "I didn't want to spend any more time than I had to with a man who smelled like he'd run five miles through the mud with a pack of hounds."

"It's been a real pleasure spending some quality time with you, too, Grove." He paused as he walked past Liza's closed door; the ice hadn't numbed everything inside him yet. "She asleep?"

"Yeah. About as soon as you hit the shower, she called the dogs in and closed the door."

Gathering the troops around her for protection. Against a man who wanted her dead? Or against the cold shoulder he'd thrown up between them and couldn't seem to breach? "Well, good night."

"Hold up." Grove crossed through the shadows. "I got a phone call while you were in the shower." The fact that he had lowered his voice to little more than a whisper couldn't be good. "A nighttime cleaning crew found Trent Jameson and his secretary dead in his office. According to the M.E., Holly Masterson, they look like professional hits."

Only hours after Liza had been in that office herself? "Our killer's already closing in."

"Looks that way."

Holden's gaze slipped to Liza's door again. Even with armed guards inside and around the house, she seemed isolated. Alone in her room with no one but her dogs to cling to for comfort. No wonder she wouldn't leave them. The emotions he'd shunned tried to fight back. "What's the plan? I know you have one."

"I'm making arrangements to move Liza to a more secure location at first light. I want her in a closed apartment with restricted access. We'll kennel the dogs at the K-9 training facility."

Isolate her even more. "She won't go for that."

"No one's giving her a choice this time." Grove had always looked like a brawny wrestler, but as he propped his hands at his hips, Holden noted that his barrel chest was thicker than usual. He was wearing a flak vest under his jacket. Armed with a Glock at his waist and a spare piece at his ankle, he was prepped for battle. Expecting the worst. "I've been working on this case for six months. The answers to your father's murder are inside her head. I want the chance to recover those answers before your father's killer shuts them down permanently. In the meantime, until the extraction team comes at dawn, I'm looking for all the reinforcements I can get."

Holden dropped his bag at his feet. "I'll get my gear."

KEVIN GROVE WAS A SNORER. No wonder, with that crooked nose that looked as though it had been busted up once or twice.

But that wasn't the sound that had snagged Holden's attention away from Grove's book that he'd picked up to read while the detective crashed on the couch for sixty minutes.

Holden hit the light button on his watch and checked the time. 2:14 a.m. Way too soon for the extraction team to arrive. The guards outside were either sitting in their cars staying warm, or farther off in the woods. The only sounds he should hear from them would come over the radio hooked to Grove's belt. And the noise he'd heard wasn't electronic.

There it was again.

A thud. Like a fist meeting a chin—only softer. The sound repeated. Again. And again.

Silently he stood, setting the book on the chair and unsnapping his Glock as he moved to the center of the room to pinpoint the source of the sound. There. He turned his ear toward Liza's bedroom door. Another thud.

Holden curled his fingers around his gun.

"Son of a…" His breath seeped out on half a curse and half a sigh of relief at the sound of tiny claws scratching the other side of Liza's door. "Damn dog."

He'd been poised and ready to strike. To shoot. To kill.

It was just a furry musketeer needing a bed of his own or a potty break.

"Cool your jets, Pee-Wee." Again, he breathed the words, unwilling to wake Grove or Liza, and hoping the dogs wouldn't wake them, either. But Bruiser must have already smelled his approach, and excitedly scratched at the door again. "I'm coming."

Thud. "Unh."

Dog? Or woman?

The sound repeated itself. *Not* the dog. Unless one of them had learned to speak. Actual words.

"Shh, baby. They'll hear."

"Parrish?" Holden opened the door. Bruiser jumped over his boot and trotted past him, heading straight for the kitchen. Holden began to push the door open farther, but hit a roadblock. He glanced down to see silver fur and an indifferent glance. "Yukon."

"Black Buick." Thud.

Ah, hell.

"Move." Yukon got up and ambled to the foot of the bed as Holden pushed his way into the room.

With his vision well-adjusted to the darkness of the house, Holden had no trouble identifying the sound now. Liza was thrashing in her bed, caught in the grip of a vicious nightmare. Her body shook. With her legs pinned beneath twisted covers and Cruiser's paws, the only thing that could move was the mattress itself. That explained the thud every time it knocked against the wall.

"Stay with me," she muttered, clutching her pillow to her stomach. "I'm trying. I'm trying."

"Liza?" The greyhound seemed frozen to the spot, either sitting on Liza to protect her mistress, or too stunned by the spasms that had disrupted her sleep to move. He shooed the dog out of the way. "Go on. Get down. I'll handle this."

Cruiser quickly obeyed, hopping down from the bed and spreading out on a pillow over in the corner.

"Liza," Holden repeated, picking up the hem of the quilt she had kicked to the floor, trying to untangle her legs without startling her awake. "Wake up, babe. It's just a bad dream." A thin sheen of perspiration dotted her skin and made a dark spot in the cleavage of her long-sleeve T-shirt. Holden eased himself onto the edge of the bed and stroked the back of his knuckles across her forehead, smoothing aside a damp fringe of copper. "It's okay, Liza. You'll be okay."

"…hate dogs. He'll shoot us. Hush…"

"Liza?" He moved his hand to her shoulder, and had to use a little muscle to hold on as she jerked. "Wake up."

Her ramblings now, her whimpers of anguish, weren't all that different from the terrified cries he'd heard coming from Trent Jameson's office during that last so-called therapy session. Was this muted suffering what her amnesia cost her? Or the aftermath of what those sessions did to her? How many times had she faced these night terrors?

No. How many times had she faced them alone?

The fist of hurt that had strangled his heart eased its grip. A lie of omission didn't seem like such a big stumbling block right now.

"Liza." He shook her. This needed to stop. "Wake up. Li—"

"No!" A fist flew at his chest. "No-o-o!"

She twisted from his grasp and sat up, fighting for her life, screaming.

"Sh, sh, sh." Holden easily absorbed the unconscious blows and quickly gathered her to his chest, pinning her arms between them and forcing her mouth against the pillow of his shoulder. "It's okay, babe, it's okay." He rocked back and forth, hugging her tight, muffling the last of her cries against his chest. "Hush now. I've got you."

"Kincaid!" The bedroom door flew open and Kevin Grove barged inside, his gun drawn—his eyes alert, his posture ready to fight.

Holden held up his hand, warning him off. "Easy."

"What the hell is going on in here?" Grove moved closer to the bed. Liza's jerk must have been as visible as the jolt he felt against his chest because Grove holstered his weapon and backed off a couple of steps. "I thought…we were under attack."

Holden wrapped his arm back around her. "Only inside her head."

"Nightmare?"

Holden nodded. He could feel the heat of her tears soaking through his sweater and the manic clutch of her fingers pinching into his skin underneath. "I've got it under control."

Liza was shaking, her breathing coming in shallow, erratic gasps. But she was finally awake, and coherent enough to apologize. "I'm sorry. I'm sorry I…woke you."

"That's okay, ma'am. Stress, I guess." Grove looked to Holden as he retreated to the door. "You got this?"

Holden nodded. As Grove closed the door behind him, Holden tunneled his fingers beneath the soft, sleep-matted fringe of hair at her nape. He massaged her gently there and rocked her back and forth. He wasn't a therapist. He didn't know what he was supposed to say or do. He just knew he wanted to make this better. "Easy, Parrish. Easy, girl. You're okay."

The stiffness of her muscles and the cold chill he could feel through her shirt and flannel pajama pants said otherwise. "I want to remember. I see the car, and the men… But every time I come close to a face, it all shuts down and all I can remember is being afraid." Her words were little more than a sob against his chest. "I'm tired of being afraid."

"I know you are. Don't think about it now. Don't think about anything at all." He held her tight, stroked her hair and continued to rock her in the darkness.

Her tears continued to fall. "I can't remember…"

"Shh." When the right words escaped him, he started humming a tune, a mournful lullaby in his throat. He dipped his head and pressed his lips to her temple and let the simple melody—one that his father had taught him long ago—be the only sound in the room.

The tears eventually stopped and the death-grip on his sweater began to relax. Minutes later, he guided her back to her pillows, smoothing her damp hair away from each freckle as he stood and pulled the sheet and quilts up to cover her.

Liza turned away and curled her legs up into a fetal position. Her eyes were closed. She wanted to sleep. But she was still shaking.

He couldn't put his own feelings to sleep, either.

With a shush of warning to the curious dogs, Holden sat back on the covers, and then lay down behind her. He slid one arm between her neck and pillow and curled the other one around her. He wrapped her up, fetal position and all, and pulled her into his body and warmth.

Resting his lips against her ear, he began to hum

again, crooning a quiet tune. He held her like that, until the shaking stopped, until her muscles relaxed—and long after, until they both settled down into a deep, healing sleep.

BLESS THE TERRIERS OF THE world for always knowing when to sound the alarm.

Bruiser's frantic bark woke Holden an instant before a window in the front room shattered.

"Hell."

Holden looped his arm around Liza's waist and rolled to the floor. "Stay down!"

"Kincaid!" Grove cursed and fired his weapon. "Kincaid, get out here!"

Liza was wide awake and nightmare-free as she yanked away the covers still tangled with her legs. "What's happening?"

"Sounds like D-Day." Holden trained his ears to identify the sounds. There was no answering report of gunshots, only the crash and smack of bullets decimating their targets inside the house. Their attacker was using a silencer or was one hell of a distance away. He palmed Liza's hip and pushed her toward her closet. "Stay close to the floor. Get your shoes on."

She nodded, then hustled across the hardwood as though she'd been to S.W.A.T. training herself. Some part of Holden grinned in admiration of that wiggling ass, but he willed the rest of him to ice over inside as he pulled his weapon and slid a bullet into the firing chamber.

"I'm comin' out, Grove!" The detective laid down a barrage of cover fire as Holden reached up to quickly turn the knob and then slide out into the living room. "What do we got?"

Grove was on the floor, using the overturned chair and coffee table as cover while he ejected his empty magazine and reloaded a fresh clip. "Shots fired on the house. At first I thought they came from the house across the street, but now I'm not sure. Every time I put my head up to pinpoint it, we get hit." He nodded toward Bruiser who bounded back and forth through the shattered glass from the door to the sofa and back, barking his fool head off the entire way. "That crazy dog heard it before I did. Damn good thing, too." He pointed toward the bullet hole ripped through the couch, just above where he'd been sleeping. He cocked his weapon. "I gotta get me a dog."

The radio on Grove's belt was buzzing with chatter. "I got nothing… from the east…our shooter's mobile…we could have more than one… Where's Molloy?"

Grove pulled the radio from his belt while Holden crawled for his own bag to pull on his flak vest and retrieve a spare. "Molloy, report!" Grove cursed at the static that answered. "Molloy! Hell. He was in the car at the north end of the street. Molloy!"

"What frequency you on?" Holden pulled out his radio and tried to reach his buddy who'd volunteered for the overtime assignment. "Dominic, this is Kincaid. Come in."

Another voice cleared the static. "He's hit, Kincaid, he's hit. Man down! Man down!"

"Son of a bitch!" Another ripple of bullets sprayed the wall above the couch. Bruiser barked. The other dogs had picked up the panic and added their voices. Holden fought like hell to keep his emotions turned off so he could focus. But his stomach was twisting into knots. His best friend. Damn it. "Dominic! I need a roll call right now!"

"This is Delgado. I'm with Molloy. He's gone."

Holden punched his fist through the drywall beside his head. Tears burned in his eyes, but he couldn't shed them.

"What's going on?" Liza's door swung open. She crawled from the bedroom with jeans and a sweater on as well as her running shoes, pulling the leashes of two dogs behind her. Still lying on the floor, she reached out toward Holden's split knuckle and the blood seeping through his fingers. "You're hurt. Kincaid?"

He snatched his hand away before she could touch him and shoved the vest at her instead. "Put this on."

Ignoring her concern, Holden rolled back to his radio. "Every man, check in."

The four surviving officers outside radioed in their location and situation, and the fact they'd lost sight of the shooter's position—if they'd ever really had it.

Grief and anger must have plugged his ears because Holden wasn't even aware of the silence until Liza asked, "Why has the shooting stopped?"

"Damn." A thin red beam of light reflected off the shards of glass on the floor and bounced up onto the ceiling. The bastard was finding his range, taking aim. "He's switched weapons. High-powered rifle!" Holden warned the others over the radio.

The first shot hit, blowing a hole the size of a cannonball in Liza's front wall. They ducked their heads as the wood splintered and plaster dust snowed down on them.

"Where's it coming from?" Holden tried to push himself up to follow the targeting laser back to its source. But the instant he raised his head, the sofa behind him was rent in two by a second shot and he dove for the floor.

"Oh, my God." That was Liza.

He propped his gun at the top of the chair and fired blindly into the night. He needed his damn rifle. "You hit?"

"No." Another shot took out a lamp. The red dot of light bounced across the back wall. "Bruiser!"

Holden rolled onto his back to see a flash of brown and tan leaping at the sofa. Bruiser barked at the laser dot, chased it back and forth. The red dot zeroed in on a patch of reddish-tan fur and stopped.

"Don't shoot my dog!"

"Liza!"

They jumped at the same time. Liza grabbed the dog and Holden grabbed Liza. Wood and metal shrapnel followed them to the floor as the sofa exploded.

"Damn it, Liza! Are you crazy?"

"Aaaah! Damn!"

Holden climbed off of Liza and the dog to see Grove clutching his left shoulder. Blood poured through his fingers. "You hit bad?"

"It went through." But the sleeve of his jacket was quickly turning red. Holden reached for the med kit in his bag. "Forget it," Grove ordered. "Get out of here."

"I'm not leaving—"

"Get out of here! He's picking us off one by one. I'm not waiting until it's just the three of us left standing."

Liza ignored Grove's tough command and pulled out a wad of gauze. While another shot tore her bedroom door off its hinges, she ripped the gauze apart and crawled over to check his wound.

Holden pulled his helmet from his gear bag and propped it up on top of the chair. He wasn't leaving Grove to be a sitting duck. With his sharpshooter's rifle and scope stored in the gun locker of the S.W.A.T. van, his improvised counterattack was going to be pretty piecemeal. But he hoped it'd be effective enough to buy them at least a few seconds of time.

"Go for it," he whispered. *Sucker.* In the few seconds it took the laser dot to track the helmet, Holden braced his Glock atop the chair and centered his aim along the red light. And fired.

He saw a blur in the distant shadows, a chimera in the night. The attacker's simultaneous shot hit wide, spinning the helmet to the floor, but missing dead center. He'd hit the scope or rifle, if not the shooter himself. "Ha! You son of a bitch—that one's for Dom."

Holden slid back behind cover and reloaded while Liza pressed the gauze to the back of Grove's wound and the detective gritted his teeth and pressed the front.

"Okay, boys and girls. I'm bettin' my next paycheck he's got a whole damn arsenal out there with him. The bullets will start flying again any second. The time to bug out of here is now."

"This will only stanch it for a little while," Liza advised. "You need to get to a doctor."

"Yeah, I'll get right on that." Grove bit down on a groan. "You must have the memories of some pretty important people inside your head, ma'am."

"Maybe just some pretty crazy ones." Plucking Holden's bandana from his back pocket, she tied the makeshift bandage into place. "If I leave, he'll come after *me,* right? He'll stop shooting police officers and come after me?"

"Probably."

She turned brave, knowing eyes to Holden. "Then let's get out of here, Kincaid."

"I thought you'd never ask."

Grove agreed. "Get her away from here until we can

regroup. Here." He pulled a pen from his pocket and wrote a phone number on Liza's pant leg. "Call me when you're someplace safe and we'll get a Plan B in motion. Are you up to protecting her on your own?"

Holden nodded. "We're going."

Grove got on his radio again. "Little Red is leaving in the Mustang in the side driveway. Let's give her cover. I repeat, Little Red is leaving."

Holden waited for one more look from Grove. "We're gonna get this son of a bitch who killed my dad and Molloy, and I hope the hell not you."

Kevin Grove laughed. "Yes, sir, we will." He nodded, then pulled himself up from behind the chair and started shooting. "Go!"

While Grove and the men outside fired almost continuously, and the sirens of KCPD backup sped toward the house, Holden snatched Liza by the back waistband of her jeans and hauled her along beside him.

He grabbed his duffel bag. She grabbed three leashes.

He had them out the side door, behind the cover of his open car door, and stuffed inside his car before the first wave of backup skidded to a halt in front of the house. A terrier, malamute and a greyhound took up a lot of space inside a little Mustang, but Holden shoved them into the backseat, pushed Liza down to the floor, and started the engine. He laid several feet of black rubber on the driveway before the spinning wheels found traction and he spun around the corner and into the night.

For the first few minutes, Holden just floored it, putting the spinning lights and shouted commands and shot-up house as far behind them as he could. He passed two ambulances that were no doubt enroute. His head had such tunnel vision that he could no longer hear the sirens. No longer hear himself even praying that Grove would survive and Molloy's death could be reversed—and that the brave woman clinging to the seat and dashboard and flying up into the air with every bump and curve might one day feel even half of the soul-deep connection that was pounding at him to keep her in his life.

There was only escape. Only speed. Only driving as fast and far as he could and hitting the open road of the highway.

Until he felt the warm hand branding his thigh. Squeezing him. Demanding his attention.

"Holden!" Liza's voice pierced the single-minded fog around his mind. She'd already called to him twice. "Holden, can you hear me?"

He blinked, clamped down on the emotions and shoved them aside before his eyes opened again. Bruiser was on the floorboards now and Liza had climbed into her seat. Thankfully, her head was still down. Yukon's puffy head was silhouetted in the rearview mirror.

"Are you okay?" he asked. "Maybe you should buckle up."

"No." She pointed to the back window. Her skin looked so pale, her hair so bright…

The dog was *silhouetted* in the rearview mirror.

"How the hell…?"

The high-beam lights of the car behind them were closing in fast.

"Get the phone off my belt. Call 9-1-1. Tell them an officer is in a high-speed pursuit on Highway 291, heading south. The shooter is no longer at Grove's location." She leaned over the center console, pushed Cruiser's curious nose aside and retrieved the phone. "Tell them officer needs assistance and that suspect is armed and dangerous. Give them my plate number." She dialed the number and recited the information as he gave it to her. "Tell dispatch the suspect's car is probably—"

"—a black Buick SUV."

Holden squinted against the blinding reflection in his mirrors. "You can see that?"

"From the other night. And…" He shifted his gaze to the firm tilt of her chin. "I remember. Parts of it. The tattooed man was driving a black Buick SUV that night. If the killers have used the same make of vehicle twice already…"

Holden nodded. "Tell Dispatch. And tell them to send backup fast."

Holden was flying down the curving interstate highway at well over ninety miles per hour. But the vehicle behind him was gaining on him fast enough that he could make out the individual headlights now. On a black vehicle. "How the hell does this guy—?"

The first shot hit a rear taillight and Cruiser leaped into the front seat. "Damn!"

Holden swerved as the big dog caught his shoulder. "Easy, girl. It's all right."

He righted the car but nearly swerved again. "No, no, no! Get down!"

Liza was pushing the seat all the way back and urging the greyhound down into the space already occupied by Bruiser. Liza pulled her legs up and moved farther back in her seat, moved higher.

The second shot pinged off the bumper and earned a deep bark from Yukon. "If he comes up here, too…"

"Get down, boy!" Liza reached back between the seats and grabbed Yukon's collar. "Get down!"

The third shot shattered the back window and Liza

screamed. Holden ignored the sting of flying glass that peppered the back of his neck. "Are you hit? Liza, are you hit!"

"No! Yukon was already down on the seat. We're all good." She pushed herself up on one elbow on the console. "You're bleeding."

"They're just cuts." Holden pressed the accelerator all the way to the floor. "I've had enough of this bastard. Take the wheel."

"Are you kidding? We're flying!"

"Take the wheel!" He unhooked the Glock at his belt. "Come on, baby, this is what I do!"

"But it's not what I…"

By the time the next shot had taken off his right sideview mirror, Liza was steering. She straddled the console and stretched her left foot over onto the accelerator, while he rolled down the window and iced his nerves.

"Be careful. Oh, God."

Her prayer disappeared in the rush of wind that whipped past his head as he turned in the seat and stuck his gun out the window. He ducked back in as he caught a flash from the side of the vehicle behind them. The perp was shooting out his side window. Driving with one hand. Making steering corrections every time they hit a curve or he fired a shot.

"Make it easy for me, why don't you."

"Kincaid? I see the Lee's Summit lights up ahead. We're going to hit some traffic."

"Keep her steady, Parrish."

He crept out the window again, bracing his arms against the car frame to help keep the buffeting force of the wind from shaking his aim. Holden lined his eye up along the barrel, inhaled his breath and held it.

Headlight or driver? Couldn't get a clear sight on the driver. Headlight. No. Tire.

"Taking the shot."

Boom.

The car behind them jerked to the left and then flipped, rolling once, twice, a third time over the grassy median until it landed upright and skidded a good thirty feet, cutting up chunks of grass and dirt before it slammed to a stop on its fractured wheels.

Holden slid back into the car and holstered his gun. He took over driving but could hold Liza's arm and balance her while she climbed back over the seat and took her place between Cruiser and Bruiser in the back. He eased his foot off the accelerator and slowed them to a more normal speed.

But before he released Liza's arm, he pulled her back toward him. "Come here."

He turned his head and stole a sweet, deep, life-affirming kiss that left him as flushed and hot as the blush on her cheeks, before releasing her and turning his attention back to the road.

"Nice driving."

"Nice shooting." She pushed the dogs aside and finally fastened her seat belt. "You're not going back to see if he's all right?"

Holden arched an eyebrow in disbelief at the question. "I want as much distance between you and that bastard as I can get. Call 9-1-1 again. Give them the mile marker and notify them of the crash. Tell them I have Little Red, and I'm taking her to a secure location."

Chapter Nine

Liza welcomed Holden's broad chest at her back and his strong arm looped around her waist as he rang his brother's doorbell. She was secure and sheltered, but there was an edginess radiating through his stiff muscles that made her wonder if she'd dreamed the caring man who'd held her while she slept.

He pounded on the frame beside the screen door. "Come on, Ed. Open up!"

Even though she hadn't seen a single car behind them once they turned off the highway and headed east through a little bedroom community and onto a gravel road that took them to this out-of-the-way acreage, Holden had insisted that she wait for him to escort her to the screened-in front porch of the gray stone house.

From the moment that first bullet had shattered her peaceful home, he'd gone into cop mode. Holden Kincaid was sexy and funny, one hell of a kisser, and he had a beautiful, mesmerizing voice whether he was crooning a lullaby or soothing her terrors with soft, meaningful words. She'd known he was a tough guy because of the guns and the uniform and the attitude, but she'd never truly seen the warrior in him until tonight.

He'd lost a good friend without shedding a tear. Shot to kill a man twice with an icy detachment. It had been downright scary to see the Jekyll-and-Hyde transformation between the man who'd put aside his own hurts to comfort her securely in his arms, and the man who stood behind her now with his gun drawn and his body positioned as a shield between her and whatever dangers still lurked in the predawn darkness.

The dogs were happy to be on solid ground and so was she. Her knees still felt more like gelatin than muscle and bone after the faceless home invasion and that wild car ride through the southeastern corner of Kansas City. But she felt as if she'd been to war, in her dreams and in her reality, and she was physically and emotionally drained.

Is that what Holden was feeling? Whatever risky, passionate emotions he'd shared in that last kiss while they were speeding down the highway, they were all bottled up inside him now. The loss of his smile and that edgy repartee that usually zinged between them added another layer of guilt onto the weight she already carried inside her soul.

Holden pulled her in tight as he knocked again. "Edward!"

The inside door swung open. Liza's breath caught in her throat and, no matter her reservations, she instinctively retreated against the wall of Holden's chest as Edward made a fantastical first impression right out of an English novel. The black screen of the storm door and the dim lighting inside intensified his brooding, unsmiling face, marked by scars and needing a shave. His hair was dark and unkempt, and his pale gray eyes glowed like a cat's in the shadows.

"You *are* on my hit list, little brother." His gravelly voice was quite unlike Holden's rich, seductive tones. He pushed open the screen door and stepped aside to let them enter. "Come on back to the kitchen. I made coffee."

She supposed she could overlook his morbid sense of humor if the man was going to offer them shelter for a few hours. Holden caught the door and nudged her in ahead of him while Cruiser, Bruiser and Yukon darted past and immediately set about investigating their new surroundings with their noses. "Thank you for letting us come."

Her effort at a cheery greeting fell on deaf ears. "Are those dogs?"

Um, yes. While Holden locked the front door, she evaluated his brother's expression and quickly decided that Edward Kincaid wasn't lacking any mental faculties, just some manners. "You don't like dogs?"

His gaze followed the dogs instead of looking at her. "My daughter always wanted a pet."

"Oh." This man had a daughter? A child lived in this remote, undecorated place? Surprise aside, some of Liza's trepidation about Edward dissipated. She'd been two years old when her parents had gotten the first pets she remembered—a calico cat named Purr, then an apricot poodle named Bobbi. She'd lived with something furry and four-legged ever since. "There are animals at shelters all over the city, waiting to be adopted. Some with dispositions that are perfect with children. At the clinic where I work, we even have this bull terrier who…"

Holden cleared his throat. When he caught her eye, he was shaking his head no, warning her to drop the subject.

Right. Not everyone appreciated a canine companion. "I can tie them up on the front porch if you want."

Edward finally looked her in the eye. She saw sadness in his, not aversion or disdain. "They're cool. Unless one of them stakes out my carpet."

"They won't." Being housebroken had always been rule one in her pack.

He nodded, resting both hands on his cane now, though she couldn't see any outward sign of injury like a cast or wrapped ankle beneath the hem of his dark jeans. "So you're the woman who saw my father's murder."

"Don't start, Edward." Holden stood beside her now, and even though he draped his arm behind her shoulders, she couldn't quite shake the chill that rippled down her spine. "It's been a long night."

Edward looked up at Holden, then studied Liza's face once more. His mouth crinkled into something she thought must be his effort at a smile. "Don't worry, Liza. My bark's a lot worse than my bite these days."

She had a feeling both could be equally dangerous. She stepped away from Holden's supportive, yet strangely cool touch. "I have partial amnesia regarding what I saw that night." She swallowed hard. This wasn't any easier to admit the second time around. "But I'm working on recovering my memories. I promise, I will do everything I can to help you. There were witnesses who stepped forward when my parents were killed. Because of them, the men responsible are now serving life in prison. I want to do the same for your family. When…when I can."

"You don't have anyone?"

She'd been braced for an entirely different question from that raspy voice—something more along the line of accusation or condemnation. Liza wasn't quite sure what he was asking. "I have my dogs." She glanced up at Holden. "And your brother. For now."

If Edward Kincaid had slapped her, she couldn't have been more surprised when he stepped forward and wrapped one arm around her shoulder in a hug. There was some deeper meaning being communicated here that she wasn't privy to. For some reason, she got the idea that this odd, unlikable man… liked her.

He tugged at the shoulder of the flak vest she still wore as he pulled away. "I think you can take this off while you're in here." When he'd released her entirely, he nodded at Holden. "He'll do right by you." He winked. "Or I'll kick his ass." The strange interchange ended and Edward limped toward the airy white kitchen at the back of the house. It appeared to be the only room where he'd turned on enough lights to see the decor. "I need coffee. Come on, little brother, let's talk. You didn't give me much to work with when you called, but I think I've got a plan."

"Will you be okay, Liza?"

"Go on."

But when she reached down to release the straps that held her flak vest in place, Holden's fingers were already there. They brushed against each other and an electric current arced between them. Liza pulled away, an instinctive reaction to a nightmare's touch, to the cold grasp of a dead man begging her to remember the truth. Or was it just a cautious reaction to a very warm, very real man who suddenly seemed like a stranger to her?

Holden's hands stilled. "Is something wrong? Look, I know Edward comes across like the Grim Reaper at times, but inside he—"

"Hush." Liza pressed her fingers to his lips to stop the unnecessary apology. When his blue eyes unshuttered and locked on to hers, she slid her hand along his stubbled jaw to cup his cheek. "You're the one I'm worried about right now. I'm sorry about your friend. And I'm sorry Detective Grove got hurt. I know it doesn't mean much, but I *will* remember. If it takes me a lifetime, I promise I will tell you who killed your father and your friend."

Holden raised his large, nicked-up hand to cover hers, and she saw a glimpse of her Dr. Jekyll again in his wry smile. "It means everything."

She would have stretched up on tiptoe and kissed him then, or wrapped her arms around him and hugged him tight.

But Edward turned on a living room lamp. "The clock's ticking, brother. You coming?"

As the shadows left the room, she saw Kevin Grove's dried blood caked beneath her fingernails. "I guess I need to wash up."

Holden pointed to a convergence of three doors off to the side of the main room. "It's the one on the left."

She pulled off the flak vest and laid it on the couch beside his before turning toward the bathroom.

"Liza?" His soft voice stopped her. His hands on her shoulders turned her. His fingers threaded into her hair and pulled her up into a needy kiss. She wound her arms around his neck and held on, held her body as close to his as she could get. He kissed her lips, her cheeks, her eyes, and then he found her mouth and kissed her again. It was bruising and hot and grieving and assuring all at once. And when he pulled away, the Holden she knew—the Holden she loved—was there in his eyes again. "We'll be all right," he promised.

Liza nodded, then pushed him toward the kitchen and went in to scrub her hands.

He might not want the love that had blossomed in her heart and was growing with every passing minute. He might not even want the passion, after a time. But she wanted to ease his hurts and regain his trust and own it for a lifetime.

And the only way to do that was to one day be able to tell him who'd killed his father.

JUST OVER AN HOUR LATER, sunrise was creeping over the horizon as Holden closed the back hatch on Edward's Jeep. They'd packed a tent, sleeping bags, a fresh box of ammo for both his Glock and rifle, and a few day's worth of food and supplies for people and dogs alike.

"Here are the keys." Edward dropped a spare set into Holden's hand and patted the vehicle's fading green paint. "Try to bring it back in one piece. I'll take care of the Mustang."

Holden nodded his thanks. "You'll call Mom and tell her where I am? What's going on?"

"As vaguely as possible, but yes."

"She'll worry if I can't call her."

"I know."

A breathless laugh sparkled in the morning air, turning the brothers' attention to Liza, who was playing a rousing game of fetch in the side yard between a windbreak of trees and the house. Her hair was the same coppery color as the oak leaves, and the damp morning chill and the robust exercise had whipped her cheeks into a rosy color. She threw a big stick and Bruiser and Yukon went charging after, while Cruiser was content to sniff the ground near Liza's feet.

It was a beautiful, normal—perfect—scene that Holden thought he could watch every morning of his life.

"I see what's to like." Edward hooked his cane over his wrist and leaned back against the vehicle, crossing his arms in front of him.

"Are you talking about the dogs or the woman?"

"Seems like they're a group package."

"They are."

Holden leaned against the side of the Jeep, matching Edward's stance. This was the brother he'd grown up with. The mentor and friend who'd taught him almost as much about being a man as their father had. He'd lost that friend on a tragic afternoon nearly two years ago—lost him to grief and the bottom of a bottle.

If there was any good thing that had come from their father's death, it might be that the loss of one good man had led to the rebirth of another. It might be a long time before Edward would ever risk his heart again—it might be never—but as far as Holden knew, since John Kincaid's funeral, Edward had stayed sober. Whether it was a testament to their father's memory, or Edward was truly beginning to heal, he didn't know. He was just glad to have some small bits of his brother back.

He only wished that the circumstances for their visit had been different, and that he could foresee more mornings like this one. But *this* was the only day he should be worrying about right now.

Holden pushed away from the Jeep and refocused his mind around the mission he had to accomplish—keeping Liza alive. "If we leave now, we can be at the camping area by nightfall."

The plan he and Edward had discussed was to hide out for a day or two in the woods along the Black River in southeast Missouri where they used to go fishing with their father and Bill Caldwell. "Stick to the back roads," Edward advised. "You know them. Try to find a spot in or near Johnson Shut-Ins State Park." The park itself had been closed due to a break in the wall of the Taum Sauk Reservoir that flooded the Black River Valley. "They've got flood damage repairs made, but they won't officially reopen the park until spring or summer. So you won't have any tourists to contend with. And if it stays this chilly, you may not even have any locals. There's a sheriff down in that area I worked on a case with. I called and gave him the Jeep's license number—nobody will stop you or ask for ID or a park fee while you're down there."

Holden nodded. "Thanks, Ed. I'll let you know when we get there and call Grove in the morning to make sure Plan B is set before I bring her back in."

"Watch your back, little brother. And watch hers. She cares about other things more than she thinks about taking care of herself."

Was that what her promise and sympathetic touch had been about earlier? Some vow to take care of him, no matter what it cost her? An uneasy decision lurked along the edge of Holden's thoughts. Was Liza's eyewitness testimony worth the risk to her mental health or even her life? She'd sounded like she'd be willing to make that sacrifice.

But would he?

Would he be content with answers if something happened to Liza? Or would losing her cripple him the same way losing what Edward loved had crippled his brother?

Love. There was that word again. Right when he thought he'd cleared the emotions out of his head and could concentrate on the job he had to do.

"Yukon? Oh, damn. Yukon!"

These few days with Liza had moved at a supersonic pace. As the dog bounded off into the trees and Liza chased after him, Holden wondered if every day of her life moved this fast. He wondered if he could keep up. He wondered at just how badly he wanted to try.

"Here, boy!" she shouted. "Yukon! Hey, a little help?"

Holden stuck his tongue behind his teeth and let loose a shrill whistle. "Yukon! Come!"

The dog halted and turned. With a shake of his shoulders that reminded Holden of a shrug of resignation, the big malamute loped straight back to the Jeep and jumped into the backseat with the other two dogs.

"Show-off." Liza jogged up behind them, looking young and fresh and nothing like the tortured soul whose nightmares had left her in agony. She shot her fingers through her hair, fluffing the copper silk into irresistible disarray. "Thank goodness he answers to you. I thought I could trust him off his leash in the unfamiliar surroundings—that he'd be less likely to run off if he didn't know where his next meal would be coming from." Catching a deep breath, she pressed a hand to her chest and beamed a smile at Edward. "Thank you for all your help."

"Thanks for asking."

In two short hours, Liza had done for his brother what no one had been able to do for nearly two years—he smiled.

Just for a moment, and then it was gone.

If nothing more ever came of their relationship, Holden would always be grateful to her for that.

Edward? Maybe not so much. He was already heading back up to the porch and waving them away. "Now give a man some peace and get out of here."

MR. SMITH TILTED HIS FACE forward and looked into the mirror, inspecting the stitched-up gash in his shaved scalp.

With distinct injuries like the long bruise across his sternum, the slight scrapes from the air bag's deployment on his face—sure indicators of an automobile accident that would never be reported—an emergency room and full-fledged doctor had been out of the question. But this after-hours clinic offered a sufficient enough facility. And, more importantly, for the right amount of money, the staff who'd worked on him could be discreet.

"It's a good look on you." Long feminine fingers gleamed against starched black cotton as his employer helped him slip into the new shirt she'd brought him. She touched one French-tipped nail to the tiny tattoo— a Cyrillic *Z*—on his right shoulder blade, where he'd branded his allegiance to her. Her reflection smiled beside him. "It's another badge of honor for you."

"A badge of honor for failing his mission?" The boss paced in the background. Though Mr. Smith was savvy enough not to dismiss the boss's influence and experience, he could feel an air of desperation in the examination room. With the click of a remote, the television above Mr. Smith's unused bed was turned off. "This *job* is all over the news this morning. A car wreck on 291. A house in the suburbs shot up by rival gangs."

Mr. Smith pulled on a silver silk tie. "Is that the spin KCPD is putting on it?" Imagine that, the work of one man, trained in stealth, with an extensive arsenal at his disposal, being credited for the work of an entire gang.

The boss was less impressed. "What I see is a lot of damage, a lot of publicity—and no dead witness. Do I need to call in someone to assist you?"

Now *that* was insulting. "Mr. Smith" had been the

code name for Z Group's top assassin for over thirty years. And he'd held the distinction longer than any of his predecessors. For one of his superiors to accuse him of losing his edge meant he was in danger of being stripped of his status. A *former* Mr. Smith had nowhere to go. Unless he moved up and became a boss.

Or he became dead.

Rich, number one and alive were all choices far better suited to his tastes.

He flicked a dimple into the perfect knot of his tie before turning to look the boss directly in the eye. "I will deal with Officer Kincaid myself. Without him, the redhead will be easy prey. Your secrets will be safe once more." And, his reputation as the best would be restored. "Did you get me the information I asked for?"

The boss nodded. "I've activated my contacts to see if we can narrow down the search. Until Kincaid calls in, we'll have to rely on deductive reasoning and track them."

A good hunt. He nearly licked his lips at the challenge. Securing a location for his assault on the safe house, including eliminating the one cop on patrol who'd seen his setup in the trees behind the neighbor's house, had been little more than a game to him. Kincaid's escape had upped the stakes and made the mission more suited to Mr. Smith's particular skills and talents.

Besides, the cop had jammed the firing pin of his favorite rifle with that crazy lucky shot from the house.

"Fine." The delay would give him a few hours to catch some shut-eye, put on a proper suit and clean his guns. "I'll need a new vehicle, as well."

"It's already in the parking lot out front. The keys are in your overnight bag." Side by side, the boss and his employer headed for the door, looking more like two business associates—or family, even—than the rivals they'd turned out to be.

Keep your friends close and your enemies closer.

Should he be concerned that the boss and his current employer could put aside their love-hate relationship and join together to turn him into the scapegoat for their dirty secrets and the dead bodies necessary to keep them?

Of course, he should. He'd put a contingency plan into place for that possibility as well.

The boss stopped at the door and turned. "Don't disappoint me."

Mr. Smith inclined his head with the slightest of nods and watched them leave. As he gathered his things and went outside to a new black SUV, he began to formulate his strategy. The redhead wasn't the issue anymore—though she was his paycheck and he would certainly get that job done. His seductive employer and powerful boss weren't even the issue. His personal mission now wasn't about Z Group or secret witnesses or covering their asses or any other damn thing.

This was personal. This was survival of the fittest. Holden Kincaid's skills and resourcefulness had proved to be almost as good as his.

Almost.

There was only one Mr. Smith.

Kincaid was good. But he was better.

He had to be.

Chapter Ten

"Penny for your thoughts." Liza strolled up beside Holden, who stood at the lip of the steep rocky bank of the Black River.

The moon was full, illuminating the path from their tent in the Ozarks, even through the canopy of tall, ancient pin oaks and evergreens. But it was cold in the moonlight, and away from the campfire, she huddled inside her sweater, wishing they'd had the time to pack winter coats. Of course, if they'd had that kind of time and opportunity, they wouldn't be roughing it like survivalists at a deserted off-season campground in the first place.

Holden was staring down into the water rushing past below their feet. Between the dark eddies and deeper currents, the water hit the big granite rocks, splashing up into the air and glittering like diamonds in the moonlight. It was a beautiful, rugged area, and she felt completely isolated from any vestige of civilization or danger.

So why was he still so quiet? "Hello? I staked the dogs out on their leashes and cleaned up all our trash. What are you doing?"

He breathed in deeply, stretching his shoulders

against his sweater, and pulling his hands from the pockets of his jeans. "I'm thinking that it's too late to catch anything tonight."

Relieved by his answer, Liza laughed. "Come on, I already made a couple of mean turkey-and-Swiss sand-wiches and even roasted marshmallows for those s'mores you ate. You are *not* thinking about fish."

"Canoeing, maybe? The river's deep enough here if you keep to the channel. Of course, when you get to the Shut-Ins," a unique formation of giant rocks that split the river into dozens of mini-waterfalls, "you'd have to carry the canoe quite a ways—"

"Wait a minute. You mean *you* in the generic sense, right? I am so not carrying your canoe for you."

That earned the beginnings of a familiar smile. "Well, we could put wheels on the bottom and hitch up Yukon. Make him do the work."

Liza shivered and hugged her arms around her mid-dle. But she wasn't ready to walk away from this com-panionable exchange just to get warm. "Are there walking or biking trails around here? I bet this is beau-tiful earlier in the autumn, when the trees are just start-ing to turn. Or in the summer. All the shade would keep things fairly cool."

"It's a great place any time of year." She felt his gaze on her and Liza tilted her chin to meet his wistful ex-pression. "My dad took us all over the state to camp and fish and hunt—"

"You shot Bambi's mother?"

He laughed. "I wondered when Dr. Animal Lover would figure that one out."

"Oh, from Day One, mister. I figured you were one of those outdoors-y tough guys. Intellectually, I understand about controlling animal populations and conservation, but I can't say it will ever be a hobby of mine." She crinkled up her face and made a confession. "I have to admit, though, that I love a good breaded catfish. My mom had a great recipe. Or some grilled walleye."

"You mean you're not a vegetarian?" He seemed properly aghast.

"Hello. I ate two of those turkey sandwiches, too." She swatted his shoulder playfully, then wound her arm through his and snuggled to his side. "Tell me about your dad and coming here."

His telling sigh quieted their laughter and brought them closer together. "Every weekend of every summer—unless one of us had a ball game or Scout camp—Dad would pack us up and take us somewhere. Mom came sometimes, but it wasn't her thing. Well, actually, I think she kind of enjoyed being outdoors, but she knew it was a guy thing for us."

"And you have three brothers, right?"

He nodded. "Sometimes, my dad's best friend from his fraternity and military days, Bill Caldwell, came with us. Man, did they have jokes and stories to tell that—" he cleared his throat "—I won't repeat."

"That good, huh?"

They stood together in the serenity of the moment for some time before Holden spoke again. "It was never about catching a fish or seeing who could build a fire without matches. It was about spending time with my dad. And my big brothers. It was about becoming a man."

"John must have been a wonderful father."

"The best. He taught us about integrity and character and loyalty. Taught us about love." She felt Holden grinning above her. "He taught me to sing, the best way to get back at Sawyer when he pulled a prank on me. He taught me to respect the land and appreciate the beauty of nature."

Holden leaned back from the link of their arms and reached down to tip her chin up. There was a drowsy longing in his expression that stirred an answering warmth inside her.

He studied her face long enough that she gave a nervous laugh. "What?"

"Thanks for listening. I miss him."

The laughter transformed into a liquid energy that filtered into her blood. "I know. I miss my folks, too. It's good to remember what was wonderful about them."

"Yeah."

"Yeah."

He drew his finger along the curve of her jaw. "Your skin's beautiful in the moonlight."

"Are you crazy? I'm a pale woman with freckles from head to toe."

"Seriously?" Within a heartbeat the mood between them changed from trading comforts to something much more intense. "You have freckles… everywhere?"

The look in his eyes changed from gentle longing to downright predatory. And daring.

Liza began a slow, knowing laugh and tried to back away. "Oh, no. No, no."

But Holden had a hold of her wrist. As she tugged away, he tugged back, pushing up the end of her sleeve. He touched his fingertip to the back of her hand. "One."

"You are not—"

"Two."

Liza tried to twist away, but he used the motion to spin her around and pull her back against his chest.

With his arm pinning her waist, he brushed the hair from her temple and touched her cheek. "Three." He touched her again. "Four." And again. "Five."

She was laughing out loud by the time he dipped his mouth to the side of her neck. "Thirteen. Fourteen."

"Stop!" She wriggled against him, rubbing her bottom over the zipper of his jeans.

He moaned against her collarbone. "Fifteen."

"Kincaid!"

He palmed her belly, sliding his hand up beneath her sweater and undershirt to brand her cool skin. "I can only count the ones I can see. I wonder if I can feel them? Hmm." He tongued the sensitive skin at the juncture of her neck and shoulder. "Or taste them."

An instant heat followed the friction of his hand and mouth, filling Liza with desire as much as laughter. "You can't—" She made a token push against his arm, but his hand slipped higher. "You can't—"

His palm settled with a possessive heat over her bare breast and Liza cried out at the instant spear of fire that went straight to her core. "I feel *that,*" he whispered in a seductive caress against her ear. He caught the aching nipple between his thumb and forefinger and squeezed and tormented the pearling nub until she wasn't laughing at all, but whimpering with need. "Liza…"

His voice was low and urgent, and it fueled something urgent inside her, too. At some point in this seduction, Liza's hands had started moving, too. She reached behind her, digging her fingers into his corded thighs and anchoring her bottom against his growing need. The rush and splash of the river filled her ears and seemed to set the pace and the fury of the blood pumping through her veins. Something blindingly hot and ultra-feminine gathered in her tingling breasts and pooled between her thighs.

"We can't…here…it's…freezing…" It was a breathless protest, a beseeching request.

He pulled his hand from her breast and turned her, forcing her to retreat as he moved forward. He bent his head and kissed her. Took another step and obliged when she tilted her mouth to kiss him again. "Run."

"What?" She was mindless with fire and want, and didn't understand.

He kissed her one last time and slipped his hand into hers. "Race you."

"Oh, no, you don't." He pulled and she followed. Their steps were awkward at first, but then she found her balance and darted ahead. His long legs stretched and easily ate up the ground to surge in front of her. She pumped her legs faster and together they reached the tent, breathless and laughing, startling the dogs and on fire for each other.

Inside the tent Liza pulled off her sweater and shirt and toed off her running shoes as Holden zipped the tent flap shut. He unhooked his belt and gun and kicked off his boots while she skimmed his sweater over his head and arms, pausing only long enough to treat herself to a taste of taut male nipple nestled in a thatch of golden brown hair.

The race continued with a crazy, fumbling effort to zip the two sleeping bags together, lose their jeans and then climb inside the giant insulated bag before the brisk autumn temperature had a chance to chill their fire.

Holden squeezed her bottom and dragged her on top of him, finding her mouth and kissing her sweetly, deeply, thoroughly, kissing her until she thought she might burst from the conflagration of heat building inside her.

"What are you doing?" Liza asked when Holden reached outside the bag to retrieve a flashlight. Surely he wasn't having second thoughts. Had he heard something? "Kincaid?"

He turned on the light, grinning like a boy who'd just discovered a whole new jar of candy. "I lost count."

He rolled her off to the side and then dove inside the sleeping bag. "Kincaid?"

She felt the nip of his teeth on her bottom. "One."

By the time Holden got to ninety-three beneath the curve of her left breast, Liza was a feverish quiver of heat and desire. Breathing hard, feeling heavy, needing him, she begged him to finish the game. "Holden. Please."

He tossed the flashlight out of the sleeping bag and crawled squarely on top of her, propping himself up on his elbows and gently stroking the damp hair off her cheek. "Say it again."

"Please."

"Say my name. Not Kincaid. Say it."

She dragged her fingers down his slick back and squeezed the curve of his muscled backside. She grinned. "Holden."

He entered her once and retreated, teasing her. Entered her again and filled her up, letting her adjust to his size and shape. She'd concede the race if he'd only grant her what she needed.

"Now, Holden."

"Yes, Liza."

He captured her mouth and moved inside her and carried them both, winners, over the finish line together.

HOLDEN LAY AWAKE IN THE DARK for some time after, his body blanketed by a beautiful naked woman, his soul replete with the kind of solace that could only come from a connection to another person that was as true and right as the link he felt to Liza Parrish.

He grieved for Dominic Molloy and his father. Railed against the injustice of having his father and best friend taken from his life by some bastard who thought they deserved to live and thrive while two good men were dead. He felt protective and possessive of, and totally humbled by the gifts this woman had given him.

Laughter. Hope. Healing.

Undeniable passion.

Unmistakable love.

They were fated to be together, meant to love—like that silly story about *Romeo and Juliet* she'd mentioned.

As he drew gentle circles across the smooth skin of her back, and the soft caress of her sleeping breath whispered across his chest, Holden vowed that their ending would be very different from the bard's version of that love story. They were going to survive this. They were going to marry and have kids—they'd have more dogs, at least. And they were going to live happily ever after.

Surely a fate that would deny him his father and best friend would not deny him this woman.

He raised his head to press a kiss to the crown of her soft copper hair. "I love you, Liza Parrish," he whispered. "I love you."

He was about to drift off to sleep himself when he felt the first jerk of her body. "Liza?"

"Shh, baby. Shush." Her words slurred against his skin.

Damn. The nightmare was taking her. He slid his

fingers to the back of her neck and tried to coax her awake. "Come back to me, babe. Come back."

"Black Buick." She shifted in his arms but refused to wake. "See you." Her whole body was quaking now, reliving the murder and terror. "Tattooed. Pinstripe. Black man. No hair."

He gave her a gentle shake as her sleepy words began to ramble. "Liza. Come on, baby, wake up."

"No." She jerked. "I see… I see you."

"Liza?"

"Pinstripe. Woman. Don't get in."

"Liza." He said her name more firmly, shook her harder. But would she feel it as some kind of attack in her dreams?

"Who…? Thank you, Mr. Smith. No-o-o!"

Enough.

Holden palmed her head to his shoulder and held her tight as she screamed herself awake.

"Easy, baby. Easy." He peppered kisses over her face and hair, absorbing the lingering aftershocks of fear that vibrated through her body.

As her pulse evened out and her breathing relaxed, Holden tried to comfort her. "Liza—"

But she pushed away and sat up straight, pulling the sleeping bag and him up with her. "It was a woman!"

He reached for his sweater and pulled it over her head to keep her warm.

"What was a woman?" he asked, wanting to pull her back into the sleeping bag to keep warm.

Perhaps sensing his intentions, she pushed the voluminous sleeves up and shoved her bangs off her forehead, avoiding his grasp. "I remembered. Maybe not all of it yet. But I remember more of that night. Maybe enough to help."

"Hold on." He raised a calming hand. "You're telling me that all the sudden, you've gotten your memory back?"

She nodded, and crawled up to sit on her knees, pulling his sweater down to cover herself in the sexiest damn version of a mini-dress he'd ever seen. "It was a woman I saw wearing the pinstriped suit. A dark-haired woman who got into the backseat of the black SUV that night. She was the only person who came out of the warehouse after I heard the gunshots. She must have killed your father."

Holden was stunned. Liza could identify his father's killer? He had to believe her. Her skin was flushed with excitement, her eyes clear. "Why do you think you're remembering this now?"

"I don't know. Maybe, after six months feeling lost inside my own head, always looking over my shoulder and wondering if that person was the killer, or that one— and never even knowing who was a threat to me and who wasn't—maybe after all that…" She reached over to frame his face between gentle hands and smiled. "I think last night, for the first time in months, I finally felt completely safe. I knew I wasn't alone with my fear anymore."

He caught one hand beneath his and turned his head to kiss her palm. "You're not alone."

She pulled away, then lifted the top of the sleeping bag and climbed into his lap. Holden was more than happy to wrap his arms around her when she snuggled against his chest. "I can also tell you a little more about the men who were with her. There was that tattooed albino—all muscle—who was driving."

"Tony Fierro." Holden nodded. Atticus had uncovered Tony's identity earlier in the year. "He was murdered in his jail cell, after my brother Atticus investigated him. Fierro tried to recover some incriminating information my father had on the people Fierro worked for."

"So he is part of your father's murder investigation."

"Yeah."

He massaged the back of Liza's neck and urged her to go on. "What else do you remember?"

"The black man. Tall. Shaved head. Nice suit. Deep voice. The woman called him 'Mr. Smith.'"

"An alias, I'm assuming?"

"Yeah. It was like a nickname." Liza paused to take a steadying breath. "She said, 'The job is finished, Mr. Smith. I know what you mean about the satisfaction of seeing your victim's eyes before you pull the trigger.'"

"Oh, God." Holden's arms convulsed around Liza at the horrific image of what his father must have suffered.

Liza wound her arms around his neck and hugged him tight. "I'm sorry. I didn't mean to hurt you. I should have said that differently."

"No." Her caring eased some of the pain. His training as a cop helped him push the rest of it aside. For now. "I need to hear everything. Exactly as you remember it. No detail is too small. So a woman killed my father. She's friends with a hit man named Mr. Smith. And they took pleasure out of what they did to my father."

"There's something more I saw this time, Holden."

"Something more?"

She pulled away, but only far enough that he could see the sorrow in her expression. "There was someone else in the car."

"A fourth person?" She'd never even hinted at that detail before.

"I couldn't get a good look at the face. But the dark-haired woman pulled something from her purse. It was a ring, I think."

Not his father's wedding ring—he'd had that on when they buried him. "Are you sure it was a ring?"

She held up her palm as if picturing exactly what she'd seen. "It was small and round and gold. She handed it to the person inside and said, 'John doesn't deserve to wear this anymore. His tattoo might say different, but he was really never one of us.'"

The slain members of Z Group had all had one thing in common—the tiny tattoo of a Cyrillic Z somewhere on their body.

"Is that important?" she asked softly.

"It could be. If we can find out who has that ring."

Chapter Eleven

Holden stopped playing with the curve of Liza's thigh where Kevin Grove had scratched his phone number onto her jeans. His senses buzzed on high alert. "What do you mean there was no body?" he asked into his cell phone. "I saw that car roll three times. If the crash didn't kill him, then he's in a hospital somewhere."

His disbelief reflected on Liza's face. "They can't find Mr. Smith?"

As the pieces of her mind began to fall back into place, there was no doubting that a professional hit man working for Z Group was after them.

Holden switched his cell phone to the other ear, forcing himself to turn away from the fearful uncertainty that made the skin beneath her freckles go pale. He wanted to pull her tight in his arms, wind the clock back seven months and pretend he had nothing to do but spend a lifetime of days like this one, sharing picnic lunches, getting better acquainted with her trim, taut body and the sassy mouth and sharp mind that went along with it.

But reality didn't work that way. He'd hoped that the people who'd murdered his father were taking some time to regroup and plan another strategy for silencing KCPD's star witness. But if the mysterious Mr. Smith was still alive, then they were out of time. If he had any connections at all, which Holden suspected he did, then he could already be tracking them. Danger and the death Mr. Smith promised could already be close by.

Holden gestured to Liza to start packing their lunch back into the cooler. She nodded and quickly went to work as he turned his attention back to the phone call. "Explain what happened."

While Grove gave him a report, Holden scanned a full 360 degrees for any sign of traffic on the park's gravel roads—or for any extra shadows moving among the trees. The detective sounded just as antsy about this whole turn of events as he was. "The air bags deployed. He was wearing his seat belt. Apparently, he walked away from the crash. I'll put Liza's description of Mr. Smith out over the wire, but…we lost him."

"Who the hell is this guy?"

"He's getting help from somewhere."

Holden's gaze was automatically drawn to the flash of Liza's copper-red hair. She was strong and sexy and savvy, compassionate to a fault and achingly vulnerable in a way that tugged at his heart and kindled an instinct to protect her that went far deeper than the badge tucked into the pocket of his jeans. Right now, *he* was the only help she had.

"Let's pack the rest of the gear," he instructed Liza.

Her gray eyes, brave but full of fear, connected with his. "He's coming, isn't he?"

He answered the rhetorical question by checking the Glock at his belt, then pulling up the right leg of his jeans to make sure the Smith & Wesson he wore in an ankle holster was loaded and ready to use. He picked up the cooler the instant she was finished and carried it to the back of the Jeep. "There's no need to panic, but we need to get moving. Grove and his men have lost track of Smith. I don't intend to make a stationary target for him."

"I'll get the dogs." Despite the sexy sway of her bottom as she jogged back to the tent, Liza was as game as any man he'd ever worked with. She might be scared—she should be—but she was keeping a level head and not allowing the emotion to cloud her thinking or question his orders.

Her cool head was a hell of a lot more conducive to survival than the irrational anger pumping through Holden's veins right now. Try as he might, the icy detachment he needed to ensure her safety just wouldn't come. This wasn't about protecting a witness any longer. Z Group had already denied him a father and a friend. He wasn't about to let them take this woman from his life. Not when he'd already opened up his heart and wedged her firmly inside.

"The press is all over this," Grove went on as Holden's gaze followed Liza's every step. "I keep directing them to the public liaison officer, but Hayley Resnick has already called me twice for a statement—about the gun fight at Liza's house and about your father's murder. She's not buying the cover that it was a gang-related shoot-out, and wants to know if I'm still working your father's case."

"Maybe she likes you." It was sarcasm meant to further the conversation.

"She's not my type."

"A gorgeous blonde isn't your type?" Holden returned to the tent, unzipped his gear bag and pulled out an extra ammo clip to tuck into his belt.

"You did get a look at my face, didn't you? Or were you too busy watching Liza's backside to notice me? I think it's more that I'm not *her* type."

"You're pretty in my book, Grove."

"Bite me." Holden could hear a murmur of voices and other phones ringing in the background, and assumed Grove had set up a command center of sorts. "Look, I ran this by Major Taylor. I know you're hiding out someplace down south—"

"We're already on the move."

"Good. We want you to hit the road back to K.C. I'm working on arrangements to get you directly into a safe house. Are the dogs—?" Bruiser barked as Liza dumped his dog food back into the sack and carried it to the rear of the Jeep. "Ah, yes. Sounds like the kids are still with you. I'll make sure we can support them at the same location as well. I owe that little terrier my life. If he wants Fifi and caviar at the safe house, he'll get it."

Holden laughed. "I'm afraid you'll have to rescue your own pooch from the pound, Grove. I don't see Liza parting with any of these guys." Bruiser ran in circles around Liza's legs and continued to bark, getting Cruiser hopping and excited as she joined the parade. But hiding out from a hit man who refused to die made laughter impossible to hold on to. "Liza remembered more details last night."

"Yeah? Let me get my notepad. Go." By the time Holden had relayed Liza's account of the fourth person in the black Buick SUV the night of his father's murder, the mysterious gold ring in the dark-haired woman's hand and her comments about "John not deserving to wear it," the dogs had become truly agitated. "Is everything all right, Kincaid?"

Liza was kneeling down now, trying to calm them, talking to the musketeers as though she expected them to understand every word she said. "What are you so fired up about? Did you see a squirrel? Come on, you two. I know this isn't our regular routine, but think of all the new smells and how much you like to ride in the car and…" Liza froze.

Like a call from his commanding officer, everything inside Holden went on alert. "What the hell?"

"Kincaid!" She grabbed the two dogs by their collars and dove for the ground as the passenger-side window of the Jeep shattered above her head.

Holden pulled his gun and ran. "We need backup! Now!"

"GET IN THE CAR! Get in the damn car!"

A second red dot of light danced through the brown grass on the ground beside her head and Liza rolled as the next shot tore up the dry leaves and dirt. "Where is that coming from?"

Why was this happening? Again. Please, God, not again!

Holden had pulled his gun and was firing blindly off into the trees to the north. Crouching low, he zigzagged back and forth, snatching Yukon by the collar and running up to her. "Move it, Parrish! Move!"

Keeping their unseen assailant pinned among the trees, he heaved the frantic-eyed malamute into the back of the Jeep.

"How did he find us?"

Holden slammed the back end shut and fired again. "Haul ass, Parrish. Talk later."

As he dashed around to start the engine, Liza obeyed,

loading the other two dogs in. She was climbing up beside them when a slash of fire burned across her right
arm. "Son of a—"

She grabbed her upper arm. For a split second she
paused and stared in disbelief at the red stripe that grew
thicker and wetter across the upper sleeve of her sweater.

"Liza!"

Holden's shout cut through her shock. As she shoved
the dogs out of her way, he grabbed her uninjured arm
and pulled her on in. Her feet were barely off the ground
when he stomped on the gas. The Jeep rocked and spun
and threw a wave of dirt and debris up behind it as the
wheels dug deep into the earth for traction. Once the
tires hit solid dirt, they shot off onto the gravel road. The
momentum threw Liza into Holden's lap and slammed
the door behind her. The dogs yelped as they were
tossed from side to side across the backseat and floor.

"Stay down!"

Holden fired out her broken window, but the instant
he stopped, a half dozen bullets pinged against the side
of the Jeep. One thunked.

"How bad are you hurt?" The butt of his gun poked
against her as he pressed his fingers into her back, checking
her from side to side for injuries while her face bobbed atop
his hard thigh. "Liza! How bad are you hurt?"

Bracing one hand against his denim-clad knee, she
tried to right herself, tried to reassure him they were still
in this chase together. "I'm okay. The bullet grazed me.
It's a long gash, nothing more. I'll be fine."

Holden pushed her cheek back down to his thigh.
"You're hit. That is *not* fine."

Another spray of bullets peppered the road behind
them and took out the back window. She lurched inside

her skin and Holden cursed. It was blue and pithy and only half of the fear and anger Liza was feeling right now. "How did he find us?"

"Pull the ammo clip from my belt," Holden ordered before answering. "I'm guessing the fourth person in that car you saw has something to do with it." Keeping her head down, Liza reached across Holden's lap and buckled him in before pulling the magazine of bullets from his waist. He did something to his gun and the spent magazine popped out onto the floorboards. He reloaded. "Can you buckle yourself in without raising up?"

Liza eased her death grip on Holden's leg and scooted backward to reach for the seat belt. Gritting her teeth against the ache that throbbed through her arm, she twisted around and secured the belt across her lap. "I'm good."

"You're doing great, babe. Just hang on to something." Holden eased a little more speed out of the racing Jeep as the sound of a powerful engine roared through the shattered windows. "Somebody has inside information. Those bastards knew where to find my dad on his Sunday morning run. Knew how to find the other Z Group members. They knew about Dad's journals."

"You mean somebody *we* trusted told him where we were hiding? Only Detective Grove and your brother Edward knew where we were, right?"

"Somebody eavesdropped or somebody told."

The growl of an engine and spit of gravel behind them grew louder. Liza grabbed the back of the seat, inching herself up to peer over the top. Black. Buick. SUV.

The driver's shaved head and dark skin were as familiar to her at sixty feet as they'd been a mere six feet away. The coldly intense expression chilled her just as deeply. "Mr. Smith. It's him—I remember him. Bald and big and—"

Holden pounded the steering wheel with his fist. "Hell!"

Liza ducked back down at Holden's curse. "What? That sounds bad. What's wrong?"

"He hit the gas tank. We're losing fuel fast. We won't make it to the highway." With a jerk of the wheel, Holden violently switched directions. The Jeep careened onto two wheels, throwing Liza into the door. They came down hard on the two airborne wheels and a terrier landed in her lap. "Here. Hold this."

Liza automatically wrapped her fingers around the gun Holden pushed into her hands. "I don't know how to—"

"Just don't shoot anything. Especially me."

His knuckles turned white as he fisted both hands around the wheel. Liza held on to both dog and gun as they left the road. Her stomach lurched as they vaulted down into the ditch and climbed up the rocks on the opposite side. "What are you doing?"

"Playing a hunch. Hoping like hell I'm right."

"About what?"

"Your Mr. Smith likes his nice suits and fancy cars? I'm guessing he's not a country boy."

"GO, GUYS! RUN! Run!"

Liza shoved the dogs away and they scattered into the trees and rocks, instinctively running away from the explosive pops of Holden's gun each time he turned to fire on the black man who pursued them.

"You're sure they'll be safe?"

"I can't guarantee anything right now, babe." He took her hand and helped her stand, leaning in to press a quick, strengthening kiss to her lips. "But we'll all make smaller, harder-to-hit targets if we split up."

She summoned a shaky smile. "I'm putting all my trust in you, Kincaid."

"Then I'll make sure I don't blow it. You ready to move out?"

Liza nodded.

They'd lost Mr. Smith and his SUV a few miles back. But the Jeep had run out of fuel and they'd been forced to move out on foot through the trees and giant rock formations that dotted the hills leading down toward the Black River. They'd paused long enough for Holden to tie his bandanna around her wound to staunch the seeping blood, and for Liza to check the dogs for injuries. Beyond a few nicks in Cruiser's hide, they were rattled by the stress of the unfamiliar situation, but basically unharmed.

She held tight to Holden's hand whenever she could and scrambled down the rocks leading toward the shutins and river below them. Sometimes she climbed, sometimes she slipped because the continuous splash of the water made the granite rocks mossy and slick. But always Holden was there to help her. To protect her. To keep her moving and alive.

Liza was a woman who was in excellent physical shape, but even she was panting from the endless descent and flat-out runs from tree to tree to rock to whatever hiding place Mother Nature offered them next. Holden led her unerringly through twists and turns, over hard-packed dirt and through icy water.

After another five minutes, Liza realized the occasional scattershot of bullets had ceased. "Holden. Holden! Wait!" She tugged on his hand to get him to slow down and stop. The cold-eyed cop was back again, searching in every direction. They were both breathing hard, wet and nearing exhaustion. She snatched up a handful of his sweater and demanded he look at her. "I don't hear him behind us anymore. Can't we rest for a minute?"

He shook his head, barely sparing her a glance. "He's not that far behind us. Going off-road bought us some time, but not much. I feel him out there somewhere. Probably watching us right now." He touched her cheek, maybe saw something in her pale features or felt something in the chill of her skin. "I'm sorry, babe. Of course, we'll rest for a few minutes." He quickly glanced around them, looking for the best hiding place, no doubt. "Here. We'll…" He froze. "Son of a bitch."

"What? Kincaid, what?"

She followed his line of sight across to the far side of the river.

Despite the mud-stained suit and the gun cradled between his hands, Mr. Smith was smiling.

"Nice try, cowboy. Now who's the best?"

He fired.

THE BULLET RIPPED through Holden's shoulder before he could even raise his gun. He heard Liza scream as he wrapped his arms around her and tumbled down into the river. He felt every rock, every branch, every painful cry from Liza before they hit the icy water and plunged down into the swift-moving current.

He kicked them back to the surface, let Liza grab a deep breath, and then pushed her under the water again. The current buffeted them from rock to rock, threatening to crack a skull or break a bone. The water chilled, stole his strength as it carried them downstream toward the giant rocks and waterfalls of the shut-ins.

Plan B sucked. His Glock was long gone and the combination of blood loss and icy temperatures were rapidly depleting his strength. He needed a Plan C. And fast. Or he was going to die. And then Liza would be all alone against a living, breathing, deadly nightmare.

He didn't want her to be alone anymore.

As they bobbed to the surface again, he was vaguely aware of laughter, then cursing. Mr. Smith must have realized that his prey was only wounded, not dead.

Not yet.

The black man scrambled along the bank above them, firing into the water.

"Hold—" Liza's words bubbled as the river rushed into her mouth. She surfaced again beside him. "Spare gun! Your leg!"

Right. Damn. Idiot.

Thank God he'd fallen for a woman who could keep her head when the world was crumbling to bits all around her.

"I love you!"

He said the words and dove beneath the water to unstrap the Smith & Wesson at his ankle. Its power was limited, but his aim would compensate if he could keep a clear head and steady hand.

He hit the next boulder with his foot, slammed into it with a bruising stop. The current pounded against his body, pinning him against the granite outcropping.

Guessing Holden's intent, Mr. Smith stopped on the bank above him, raised his weapon and trained the red laser dot center mass of Holden's chest.

Liza sailed on past as Holden raised the gun out of the water and lined the bastard up in his sights. Pain exploded in his side as he pulled the trigger.

LIZA TIED YUKON'S lead around Holden's wrist and commanded the dog to pull. "Come on, Yukon. Go! Pull, big guy. Pull!"

Yukon sat on the bank while she shivered. Liza was exhausted, too weak to pull Holden's unconscious body out of the water. He'd lost so much blood. In addition to being shot twice, he'd hit his head on one of the rocks when the kick of the gun had cost him his balance in the rushing water.

But Mr. Smith was dead, lodged in the rocks on the bank somewhere upstream.

She was free. She was safe.

But Liza was so tired. And Holden was so hurt.

"Damn it, dog. I saved your life. Don't you think you owe me one? Please."

Then Holden whistled. A shrill, loud, wonderful sound that hurt her ears and warmed her heart. "Move it!"

Obeying the voice she wanted to kiss with relief, the big malamute clawed at the mud and slipped back toward the river, but then his back paw hit solid rock and she felt a tug on the leash. "Come on, boy. Come on."

"Yukon, pull!" Holden's voice was stronger now.

Yukon leaned into his collar and pulled. And pulled. Holden's arm came around Liza's waist as she found her footing and used what little strength she had left to help him.

When they were securely on dry land, Liza freed Holden's wrist. "Good boy. Good boy."

She wanted to hug the dog, but she was too exhausted to spare time for anything more than to press her hand to the wound in Holden's side. The movement of the water must have deflected Smith's shot to a less vulnerable region of the body, but she knew that a bullet could ricochet inside the body and do more damage than the entry wound itself.

"You're not going to die on me, are you, Kincaid? Kincaid?" Liza grunted with the strain of turning him, while Holden bit down on a moan. She probed and bent her ear to his chest and back to check his breathing, then checked his pulse. Finally, she pulled her shirt off from beneath her soggy sweater and created a makeshift bandage. When her shaking fingers and lack of medical supplies could do no more, she collapsed beside him on the riverbank. "Your shoulder wound just caught the flesh, nothing vital. It looks like the bullet is still inside. But your breathing is steady and I don't hear fluid inside the chest cavity, so I don't think it nicked a lung. The cold water might actually be a blessing. The temperature must have slowed your heart rate, so the bleeding isn't too severe. I'm used to treating dogs, not men, but I think if you don't move too much before I get you to an E.R., that—"

"I'll live." He pulled her into his arms and kissed her hard, then fell back to the ground to rest beside her. He snapped his fingers and Yukon ambled over to sit beside them.

"Lie down, you mutt." The dog lay down beside him, sharing the warmth of his body and finally offering his allegiance to the pack. "I'm sure my cell phone is shot. But there's a radio in the Jeep. If we can hike back to it, we should be able to call the local sheriff."

Hike? Liza's weary sigh came all the way from her freezing toes. "In a minute, okay?"

"Okay."

Bruiser and Cruiser joined them. Soon enough, they'd be rested and warm enough to think about doctoring wounds and making phone calls and living their lives.

Liza marveled at the way Holden had tamed Yukon, and the strong bond the two shared. She cuddled closer, understanding why the dog would want to bond with this man. "You just called my dog a mutt, Kincaid. And after he saved your life."

"*My* dog, Parrish. Yukon is *my* dog."

Yes, he was. And as they lay on the bank, warming in the sun, Liza rested her cheek against Holden's heart and hugged him as tight as her weary arms and his injuries would let her. "I'm yours, too."

Chapter Twelve

Holden Kincaid wasn't the first gunshot victim the Truman Medical Center had ever treated, but he might well be the most popular. Even in the middle of the night, long after official visiting hours had ended, he sat up against a stack of pillows, winked at the nurse who'd come to change his IV drip and promised he intended to get some rest.

He'd survived a freezing river, a bullet in his gut, nearly losing Liza to a hit man, being life-flighted to Kansas City and surgery to remove said bullet and stitch him up inside and out. He was beat up, he was beat. But he could survive a few more minutes with his friends and family creating a hushed, friendly chaos around him.

And he could damn well survive until somebody let him see with his own eyes that Liza had survived her injuries as well, and was merely being kept overnight in the same hospital for observation. His mother sat on a chair beside his bed, and he squeezed her hand a little more tightly, just thinking about how much he missed Liza and how much he worried about how safe she really was when out of his sight.

Susan Kincaid squeezed right back. "Are you in pain, sweetie?"

"I'm okay." The tenderness of the surgery and bandages that held him together didn't ache too much unless he tried to move that side of his body. But even the sharp twinge that stabbed through his gut when he adjusted his position on the bed was nothing compared to the uncertainties about Liza roiling inside him.

"I'm yours," she'd said. But he'd been in and out of consciousness beside that river. Was she his for that moment? For as long as she was in danger and needed him? Was it forever? Or had he just dreamed what he wanted to hear?

It gave him a pretty clear understanding of the doubts and second-guessing Liza must have suffered through when her memory had been on the fritz. He didn't like not having the answers he needed. Didn't like it one damn bit.

Sensing his discomfort if not entirely understanding the cause of it, his mother pushed her chair back and stood, silencing the chatter in the room with a stern maternal look that could have commanded an entire police force. "Gentlemen? Visiting hours just ended. You can come back and see Holden in the morning. He needs to get some sleep."

"Yes, ma'am." With a flurry of similar responses, Holden's precinct commander, Mitch Taylor, and his S.W.A.T. team leader, Lieutenant Cutler—along with his buddies Rafe Delgado and Trip—left the room with handshakes, commiserations about Dominic Molloy, good wishes and gibes about getting out of work for a few weeks.

Bill Caldwell rose from his chair in the far corner and came to wrap an arm around Susan's shoulders. "Does that mean me, too?"

She reached up and patted his hand where it rested

alongside her neck. "You might as well, Bill. I'm going to stay the night and keep an eye on my baby boy."

"Mom…" Holden's token protest at being labeled the "baby" of the family when he towered over everyone but Sawyer quickly faded beneath the love and concern shining from her eyes. "Thanks for looking out for me."

"It's a mother's prerogative." Her wink made him smile.

Bill leaned in and kissed Susan's cheek. "Then I'll be going." He reached out to shake Holden's hand. "You feel better soon, son. I don't like seeing your mother get scared like she was today."

"Bill—"

"She might not show it. But you four boys are everything in the world to her." He kissed her again. "I'll see you in the morning for breakfast?"

A breakfast date? Susan nodded. "Good night."

But before Bill could open the door, all three of Holden's older brothers filed back into the room.

"Hang on a minute, Bill," Atticus said. "We need to talk."

The older gentleman laughed. "That sounds ominous."

There *was* something slightly ominous about the late night visit that made Holden grit his teeth against the pain in his gut and sit up straighter. Sawyer, Atticus and Edward—even with his cane to lean on—standing side by side at the foot of the bed created a daunting wall of don't-mess-with-me attitude. They were on to something. And the one thing that had united all four brothers—four different kinds of men, four different kinds of cops—and put them on a single mission was solving their father's murder.

"What's up, guys?" Holden prodded.

Sawyer circled the bed and wrapped Susan up in a

bear hug and a kiss. "If you don't mind, Mom, we need to have a private conversation."

Once her feet were back flat on the floor, her narrowed gaze took in all four of her sons. "Man talk or police business?"

The grim looks meant police business.

"I see." She turned and smiled at Holden. "How about I go check on Liza Parrish. The doctor said her medical treatment in the field stabilized you enough to make it into surgery. I think I owe her a personal thank-you." She squeezed a hand or kissed a cheek of each man as she made her way to the door Atticus held open for her. "Behave yourselves. Holden needs his rest."

"Thanks, Mom."

Atticus didn't waste any time getting down to business as soon as the door closed. He pulled his reading glasses and cell phone from his suit jacket to read the information he'd stored there. "I got a message from Holly Masterson at the crime lab. She's doing an autopsy on your Mr. Smith to try to get an ID on him, and see if they can match him to anything at Dad's crime scene."

Sawyer had apparently been talking to Dr. Masterson as well. "Some of her lab files, including Dad's case, have been corrupted by a computer hacker—we suspect by one of the cons who escaped prison with Mel's ex-husband six months ago. At any rate, she's having her people retest the evidence they have on hand to rebuild the facts of the investigation."

Pulling off his glasses, Atticus continued. Apparently, while Holden had gone on the run with Liza, his brothers had been busy. "Dr. Masterson also told me that preliminary reports indicate the bullet they took out of you, little brother, is a disintegrator, matching the ones they took out of Dad, James McBride, and the Jane Doe at the dump I investigated earlier this year."

Edward had been silently hanging back until now. "Tell them about your hunch, A."

"I've asked Dr. Masterson to run a DNA comparison against my Brooke to see if the Jane Doe could be her mother, Irina Zorinsky Hansford." Holden remembered that Atticus and his fiancée, Brooke Hansford, had traveled to Sarajevo to move her parents' bodies back to the States from where they had been buried after a car wreck when she was still a baby. But the body in the mother's grave had turned out to be someone else. Had Brooke's mother, once a government agent who'd worked with John Kincaid, staged her own death? Or had someone moved the body to cover up a different crime?

Did the Jane Doe in the city dump or the dark-haired woman Liza had seen at the warehouse the night of John Kincaid's death have anything to do with missing mothers or the twisted cover-up that had prompted their father's murder?

But Bill Caldwell had picked up on a different oddity in the conversation.

"Disintegrating bullets?" he questioned skeptically. "Bullets composed of an alloy that breaks down in the body's tissues so that it can't be traced? That sounds like something we were developing in the test section of Caldwell Technologies. But there were only prototypes. They had no commercial value, so we halted production."

"No legitimate commercial value," Atticus pointed out. "But an untraceable bullet would be a big seller on the black market."

"Had any security leaks lately?" Holden's sarcasm asked a very real question.

"No. None that I know of. And I know my company. I'll still have my security team look into it ASAP, though." Bill nervously twisted the ring on his finger as he looked from Holden to Sawyer, who'd moved in right beside him. But Caldwell hadn't built himself a wealthy technology empire by backing away from suspicion or confrontation. The movement of his hands stilled and he pulled his shoulders back. "You're not saying I had anything to do with your father's murder, are you? He was the best friend I ever had. You four are like sons to me. And your mother is… becoming very special to me."

Though Holden wasn't completely comfortable with Bill's growing relationship with their mother so soon after their father's death, this conversation was about the case, not changing family ties.

Atticus tucked his glasses back inside his jacket. "You knew Irina Hansford, didn't you?"

"Why would I know a woman from Yugoslavia? It's not even a country anymore."

Sawyer pushed further. "Thirty years ago, you and Dad weren't just in the military together—you both worked for a covert agency called Z Group. Along with James McBride and Leo and Irina Hansford."

Bill's expression tightened into a poker-player's mask. He held up his left hand to point out the gold fraternity ring he wore. "Your father and I were in the same fraternity in college. We went through ROTC—"

"Don't lie to us," Holden interrupted. He might not have been in on the discussion outside his room, but he knew where his brothers were going with this. "If Dad

really was your best friend, you'll give us straight answers, even if you've been sworn to silence. Our father
found out that Z Group was still in existence—thirty
years after it was supposedly disbanded by the government. Only now they've turned into a bunch of arms and
intelligence dealers. Somebody killed Dad—a woman,
I believe—to keep the secret."

"You think John was murdered by a woman?" Bill's
blank expression became a frown of confusion. "Then
why am I under attack here? If someone in my company
is responsible for supplying the weapons and ammuni-
tion that killed these people, then I'll look into it. I want
to find John's killer as badly as the rest of you."

"KCPD can do that." Edward pushed Atticus aside
to face Bill directly across Holden's bed. "We need you
to drop the innocent facade and tell us everything you
know about Z Group."

LIZA KNOCKED SOFTLY at Holden's door, bringing an
abrupt end to the conversation on the other side.

"Come in."

The door jerked from her hand as a dark-haired gentleman with silver sideburns appeared in the opening.
"Excuse me."

"Excuse…" But there was no need for her to apologize. His expression tense with an emotion that passed
by too quickly to name, the man lengthened his stride
and headed down the hall toward the elevators. Recovering from the startle, Liza pulled her hospital-issue
robe together at the neck and snugged the tie belt at her
waist. She swallowed hard, steeling her nerves and
hoping that Susan Kincaid had been as accurate about
her advice as she'd been sincere when she'd suggested

that, since Liza was still awake herself, Holden would welcome a visit from her.

She stepped into the softly lit room. He already had three visitors—tall, dark-haired men—but her eyes were instantly drawn to the bruised face of the man sitting up in bed. Holden looked tired, pale against the crisp white sheets. His square jaw needed a shave. The faded hospital gown stretching from shoulder to shoulder seemed thin and insubstantial against the hospital's sterile, cool air. But that piercing blue gaze—blessedly clear and locked on to hers—made her insides knot up in a bundle of feminine awareness and heartfelt need. "Hey, Kincaid."

"Parrish."

She took another step into the room, glancing from one man to the next. "If I'm interrupting something important, I can come back in the morning."

"No." Holden's deep voice cracked, but his gaze never wavered from her. "They were just on their way out."

"But I thought we were going to compare our notes and—"

"Atticus." The biggest Kincaid brother, whom she'd learned was Sawyer, moved his gaze from the executive-looking one to Holden and back. "Think about it, smart guy. We can finish this tomorrow."

"Of course. I understand a man's priorities." After saying goodbye to Holden, Atticus turned to the door. He paused for a moment in front of Liza, then dipped his head and kissed her cheek. "Good to see you in one piece, Miss Parrish."

"Thanks. I—"

Sawyer picked her up and squeezed her in a hug before Atticus was out the door. He was warm and big and gentle as could be. "Glad I can finally do this." By the time he set her feet back on the floor she was too stunned to speak. "Keep my baby brother out of trouble, okay?"

"Liza." Edward nudged Sawyer out the door. His steely gray eyes lingered on her face for a moment before his chin dipped in a nod. Thanking? Approving? Of what? But he exited without saying another word.

As the door closed softly behind her, Liza thumbed over her shoulder and crossed to the foot of the bed. "What just happened?"

Holden's weary expression relaxed with a grin. "It's a Kincaid thing."

"Meaning?"

"Meaning they like you. Now get over here." He stretched out his hand toward her. "I'll probably rip some stitches if I leap out of bed at this point. I have something I want to talk to you about."

With a smile, Liza hurried to his side and clasped his hand between both of hers. "No leaping, okay? You've scared me enough for one day."

"The doc says I'm going to be okay," he reassured her. He stroked his thumb over the back of her knuckles, warming her entire body with the subtle gesture. "Who's watching the musketeers?"

"Believe it or not, Detective Grove volunteered to take them for the night. His apartment is going to be pretty crowded, but he seems to enjoy the company. In fact, I think he may be visiting our shelter to adopt a dog of his own soon." Liza turned her hands to halt the distracting caress of his thumb. She looked straight into his blue eyes and sought an answer. "What do your brothers know that I don't? Does it have to do with my testimony? I'm writing down everything I remember. And more and more details keep coming. My attending physician here gave me a list of reputable counselors I could talk to about memory loss. He thinks I'm at a point now where I'll remember all of it, eventually."

"That's great."

If not the murder investigation, then what had Holden and his brothers been discussing? And why wouldn't he look away? She began to feel a self-conscious blush creeping into her cheeks at his unblinking study of her. "You're not worried about me still, are you? Mr. Smith is dead and there are guards posted outside my room. You've got a trio of cops lurking outside of yours, too."

A plastic IV tube followed his hand as Holden reached out to brush a wisp of hair off her cheek. "I think I'm always going to worry about you."

Sweet. But he was stalling. "Spit it out already, Kincaid."

Holden looked deep into those silvery eyes. How could one woman be so beautiful, so brave, so stubborn and caring all at once? Freckles and copper hair, strength and sass, and a determination to do the right thing were proving to be an irresistible combination to him. Liza Parrish was a wake-up call to his heart and his life, and he always answered when he was called to a mission. "You love me, right? Because I'm 99.9 percent sure I'm in love with you."

Half a laugh and a wry smile made his heart pound faster. "Only 99.9, huh? So there's a tenth of a percent of you that's not sure?"

"No. I love you." The teasing came as naturally as the need to touch her. He feathered his fingers into the silky copper at her temple. "But I don't want to come on too strong."

He detected a glitch in her smile. "We've only known each other for a few days," she said.

"Doesn't matter." He pulled her toward him, urging her to sit on the bed facing him. "My job requires me to turn off my emotions and pretend I don't feel a damn thing. But I haven't been able to do that with you. I tried to make protecting you part of the job, part of my dad's murder investigation. But I can't. What I feel for you— it's personal. It's real. And it's not going away. I know my family comes on like gangbusters, and you don't have anybody and you may be a little reticent to—"

She pressed her fingers to his lips. "Shut up, Kincaid. I'm not alone. I haven't been since I met you."

"Yeah, well I don't want you to confuse gratitude with…" The stern look in her expression eased the last of his doubts. They were going to be okay. His memory hadn't played tricks on him. "Shutting up now."

"I have Bruiser, Cruiser and Yukon—okay, so Yukon is a traitor and has adopted you instead of me." He kissed her fingertips as she pulled them away, then returned the favor by turning her warm lips into his palm where it rested against her cheek. "When I couldn't remember things, I didn't trust my own thoughts and feelings, much less allow myself to trust anyone else. But my dogs trust you. And they're the best judges of character I know. If they can believe in you, I can, too."

Holden wanted her closer. Wanted her in his arms, now. But he sensed that she needed to talk this out. "Coming from anybody else, that'd be a really cornball thing to say," he said. "But I know how you feel about the musketeers. I guess I've developed a soft spot for them, too. I'm glad I've earned everyone's trust."

"You've earned more than that." She inched a fraction closer and his pulse throbbed with hope. "I wasn't sure I wanted to give my heart to anybody ever again—I've been in tough-chick survival mode for a long time. But you didn't leave me any choice." She framed his jaw between her hands. *Say it, babe. Believe it.* "I love you, Holden. I'm in love with you."

"Works for me." The stitches in his side offered barely a twinge as he wrapped his arms around her and pulled her in for a long, leisurely, thorough kiss. When he finally came up for air, Liza was clinging to his neck, her faced flushed and smiling. Holden rested his forehead against hers. "So, if I want this connection we've made to go on forever, you'd be okay with that?"

"I'd be very okay with that."

"And say I wanted to marry you, would there be someone I should ask?"

"Besides me?"

"I know your parents are gone. Is there any other family…? Oh." She was grinning as she crawled beneath the covers with him, tenderly finding a spot where she could snuggle against his uninjured side. Holden wound his arms around her and tucked her healing, loving warmth even closer. "Fine. I'll talk to the dogs as soon as I'm out of here."

* * * * *

Look for the exciting conclusion to
THE PRECINCT:
BROTHERHOOD OF THE BADGE *miniseries*
with Edward's story, KANSAS CITY CHRISTMAS.
Coming next month. Only from Harlequin Intrigue.

Here's a sneak peek at THE CEO'S CHRISTMAS PROPOSITION, the first in USA TODAY bestselling author Merline Lovelace's HOLIDAYS ABROAD trilogy coming in November 2008.

American Devon McShay is about to get the Christmas surprise of a lifetime when she meets her new client, sexy billionaire Caleb Logan, for the very first time.

Silhouette
Desire

Available November 2008

Her breath whistled out in a sigh of relief when he exited Customs. Devon recognized him right away from the newspaper and magazine articles her friend and partner, Sabrina, had looked up during her frantic prep work.

Caleb John Logan, Jr. Thirty-one. Six-two. With jet-black hair, laser-blue eyes and a linebacker's shoulders under his charcoal-gray cashmere overcoat. His jaw-dropping good looks didn't score him any points with Devon. She'd learned the hard way not to trust handsome heartbreakers like Cal Logan.

But he was a client. An important one. And she was willing to give someone who'd served a hitch in the marines before earning a B.S. from the University of Oregon, an MBA from Stanford and his first million at the ripe old age of twenty-six the benefit of the doubt.

Right up until he spotted the hot-pink pashmina, that is.

Devon knew the flash of color was more visible than the sign she held up with his name on it. So she wasn't surprised when Logan picked her out of the crowd and cut in her direction. She'd just plastered on her best businesswoman smile when he whipped an arm around her waist. The next moment she was sprawled against his cashmere-covered chest.

"Hello, brown eyes."

Swooping down, he covered her mouth with his.

Sheer astonishment kept Devon rooted to the spot for a few seconds while her mind whirled chaotically. Her first thought was that her client had downed a few too many drinks during the long flight. Her second, that he'd mistaken the kind of escort and consulting services her company provided. Her third shoved everything else out of her head.

The man could kiss!

His mouth moved over hers with a skill that ignited sparks at a half dozen flash points throughout her body. Devon hadn't experienced that kind of spontaneous combustion in a while. A *long* while.

The sparks were still popping when she pushed off his chest, only now they fueled a flush of anger.

"Do you always greet women you don't know with a lip-lock, Mr. Logan?"

A smile crinkled the skin at the corners of his eyes. "As a matter of fact, I don't. That was from Don."

"Huh?"

"He said he owed you one from New Year's Eve two years ago and made me promise to deliver it."

She stared up at him in total incomprehension. Logan hooked a brow and attempted to prompt a non-existent memory.

"He abandoned you at the Waldorf. Five minutes before midnight. To deliver twins."

"I don't have a clue who or what you're..."

Understanding burst like a water balloon.

"Wait a sec. Are you talking about Sabrina's old boyfriend? Your buddy, who's now an ob-gyn doc?"

It was Logan's turn to look startled. He recovered faster than Devon had, though. His smile widened into a rueful grin.

"I take it you're not Sabrina Russo."

"No, Mr. Logan, I am *not*."

* * * * *

Be sure to look for
THE CEO'S CHRISTMAS PROPOSITION
by Merline Lovelace.
Available in November 2008 wherever books are sold,
including most bookstores, supermarkets, drugstores
and discount stores.

Travel back to Skull Creek, Texas—
where all the best-looking men
are cowboys, and some of those
cowboys are *vampires!*

USA TODAY bestselling author
Kimberly Raye ties up her
Love at First Bite trilogy with...

A BODY TO DIE FOR

Vampire Viviana Darland is in Skull Creek, Texas,
looking for one thing—an orgasm. Or more
specifically, the only man who'd ever given her
one, vampire Garret Sawyer. She knows her end
is near, and wants one good climax before she
goes. And she intends to get it—before Garret
delivers on his promise to kill her....

Paranormal adventure at its sexiest!

Available in November 2008 wherever
Harlequin Blaze books are sold.

nocturne™

ESCAPE THE CHILL OF WINTER WITH TWO SPECIAL STORIES FROM BESTSELLING AUTHORS

MICHELE HAUF

AND

VIVI ANNA

WINTER KISSED

In "A Kiss of Frost," photographer Kate Wilson experiences the icy kisses of Jal Frosti, but soon learns that this icy god has a deadly ulterior motive. Can Kate's love melt his heart?

In "Ice Bound," Dr. Darien Calder travels to the north island of Japan, where he discovers an icy goddess who is rumored to freeze doomed travelers. Darien is determined to melt her beautiful but frosty exterior and break her of the curse she carries...before it's too late.

Available November wherever books are sold.

REQUEST YOUR FREE BOOKS!

2 FREE NOVELS PLUS 2 FREE GIFTS!

HARLEQUIN®

INTRIGUE®

Breathtaking Romantic Suspense

YES! Please send me 2 FREE Harlequin Intrigue® novels and my 2 FREE gifts (gifts are worth about $10). After receiving them, if I don't wish to receive any more books, I can return the shipping statement marked "cancel." If I don't cancel, I will receive 6 brand-new novels every month and be billed just $4.24 per book in the U.S. or $4.99 per book in Canada, plus 25¢ shipping and handling per book and applicable taxes, if any*. That's a savings of close to 15% off the cover price! I understand that accepting the 2 free books and gifts places me under no obligation to buy anything. I can always return a shipment and cancel at any time. Even if I never buy another book from Harlequin, the two free books and gifts are mine to keep forever.

182 HDN EEZ7 382 HDN EEZK

Name	(PLEASE PRINT)
Address	Apt. #
City	State/Prov.	Zip/Postal Code

Signature (if under 18, a parent or guardian must sign)

Mail to the **Harlequin Reader Service:**
IN U.S.A.: P.O. Box 1867, Buffalo, NY 14240-1867
IN CANADA: P.O. Box 609, Fort Erie, Ontario L2A 5X3

Not valid to current subscribers of Harlequin Intrigue books.

Want to try two free books from another line?
Call 1-800-873-8635 or visit www.morefreebooks.com.

* Terms and prices subject to change without notice. N.Y. residents add applicable sales tax. Canadian residents will be charged applicable provincial taxes and GST. Offer not valid in Quebec. This offer is limited to one order per household. All orders subject to approval. Credit or debit balances in a customer's account(s) may be offset by any other outstanding balance owed by or to the customer. Please allow 4 to 6 weeks for delivery. Offer available while quantities last.

Your Privacy: Harlequin is committed to protecting your privacy. Our Privacy Policy is available online at www.eHarlequin.com or upon request from the Reader Service. From time to time we make our lists of customers available to reputable third parties who may have a product or service of interest to you. If you would prefer we not share your name and address, please check here. ☐

HI08R

Inside ROMANCE

Stay up-to-date on all your romance reading news!

The Inside Romance newsletter is a FREE quarterly newsletter highlighting our upcoming series releases and promotions!

Click on the <u>Inside Romance</u> link on the front page of **www.eHarlequin.com** or e-mail us at insideromance@harlequin.ca to sign up to receive your FREE newsletter today!

You can also subscribe by writing us at: HARLEQUIN BOOKS Attention: Customer Service Department P.O. Box 9057, Buffalo, NY 14269-9057

Please allow 4-6 weeks for delivery of the first issue by mail.

IRNBPA208

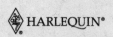

HARLEQUIN®

INTRIGUE®

COMING NEXT MONTH

#1095 CHRISTMAS AWAKENING by Ann Voss Peterson
A Holiday Mystery at Jenkins Cove
The ghost of Christmas present looms over Brandon Drake when his butler's daughter returns to Drake House. Can Marie Leonard and the scarred millionaire find answers in their shared past that will enable them to catch her father's killer?

#1096 MIRACLE AT COLTS RUN CROSS by Joanna Wayne
Four Brothers of Colts Run Cross
When their twins are kidnapped, Nick Ridgely and Becky Collingsworth face the biggest crisis in their marriage yet. Will the race to save their children bring them closer in time for an old-fashioned Texas Christmas?

#1097 SILENT NIGHT SANCTUARY by Rita Herron
Guardian Angel Investigations
When Leah Holden's seven-year-old sister goes missing, she turns to detective Kyle McKinney. To reunite this family, Kyle will do anything to find the child, even if it means crossing the line with the law...and with Leah.

#1098 CHRISTMAS CONFESSIONS by Kathleen Long
Hunted by a killer who's never been caught, Abby Conroy's world is sent into a tailspin, which only police detective Gage McDermont can pull her out of. One thing is certain: this holiday season's going to be murder...

#1099 KANSAS CITY CHRISTMAS by Julie Miller
The Precinct: Brotherhood of the Badge
Edward Kincaid has no reason to celebrate Christmas—until he begins playing reluctant bodyguard to Dr. Holly Robinson. Now, the M.E. who can bust the city's biggest case wide open might also be the only one able to crack Edward's tough shell.

#1100 NICK OF TIME by Elle James
Santa's missing from the North Pole and his daughter, Mary Christmas, can't save the holiday by herself. It's up to cowboy and danger-junkie Nick St. Clair to find the jolly ol' fellow in time for the holidays, before Christmas is done for as he knows it....